GOING HOME

GOING HOME

June Thomson

CHIVERS
THORNDIKE

This Large Print book is published by BBC Audiobooks Ltd, Bath, England and by Thorndike Press®, Waterville, Maine, USA.

Published in 2006 in the U.K. by arrangement with Allison & Busby Limited

Published in 2006 in the U.S. by arrangement with Allison & Busby Limited

U.K. Hardcover ISBN 10: 1–4056–3830–3 (Chivers Large Print)
                ISBN 13: 978 1 405 63830 2
U.K. Softcover ISBN 10: 1–4056–3831–1 (Camden Large Print)
                ISBN 13: 978 1 405 63831 9
U.S. Softcover ISBN 0–7862–8975–9 (British Favorites)

The text of this Large Print edition is unabridged.
Other aspects of the book may vary from the original edition.

Set in 16 pt. New Times Roman.

Printed in Great Britain on acid-free paper.

British Library Cataloguing in Publication Data available

Library of Congress Cataloging-in-Publication Data

Thomson, June.
    Going home / by June Thomson.
       p.   cm.
    "Thorndike Press large print British Favorites."
    ISBN 0–7862–8975–9 (lg. print : sc : alk. paper)
    1. Police—England—Fiction. 2. Missing persons—Fiction.
    3. Large type books. I. Title.
    PR6070.H67G65 2006
    823'.914—dc22   2006024958

Part One

MEMORANDUM

Date: Wednesday, 27th August 2003
To: Detective Chief Inspector Jack Finch
From: Detective Sergeant Helen Wyatt

As requested, here is a printout of the transcript of the manuscript pages found in the attic of Alex Lambert's house, Field Lodge, Foxton Road, Northorpe, Essex on 22nd August 2003.
For easier reference, I have numbered the pages but have presented it in its original format, that is as a continuous narrative.

JOURNAL

Monday, 2nd June.
Yesterday I came face to face with someone who reminded me so strongly of M that it was like meeting his ghost, as if M had been resurrected and had come back again after all these years to haunt me, a ridiculous comparison because, on reflection, the two men are physically quite dissimilar. All the same, the encounter has disturbed me considerably and I can't get it out of my mind.
It was Jocelyn who introduced us and, as soon as she telephoned me, I knew something had happened to excite her. She didn't

mention Charlotte as she usually does in that sweetly sincere voice she always uses when she refers to my daughter. 'And how's darling Charlotte?' she asks, her mouth too close to the phone so that she sounds intimate and soft and full of genuine concern.

It always angers me. She makes it seem as if Charlotte is severely brain-damaged instead of being my bright, beautiful, fourteen-year-old daughter who just happens to be profoundly deaf.

I always reply in a brisk, matter-of-fact manner. 'Oh, she's fine,' I say, hoping to convey by my voice that I won't have Charlotte pitied, and that she can't get closer to me through my daughter.

But Jocelyn never picks up the nuances of a conversation.

'Oh, do give her my love,' she says, putting a special breathy emphasis on the last word, meaning, of course, that her love is really intended for me.

'Thanks, I will,' I reply shortly.

But on Wednesday when she rang, there was no reference at all to Charlotte. She sounded different, too; louder, her voice excited and higher pitched, as if she had important and wonderful news to tell me, although apparently the only reason she'd phoned me was to invite me round for pre-lunch drinks on Sunday, that is yesterday morning.

'At eleven,' she said. 'You'll be able to come,

won't you?'

I hesitated. I try to avoid meeting her as much as I can; I don't want her, or anyone else come to that, to think of us as an item. And I guessed she had deliberately chosen that particular Sunday morning because she knew Charlotte wouldn't be with me. She only comes home from her boarding school every other weekend.

'Oh, do say yes,' Jocelyn urged. 'There's someone I'm dying for you to meet.'

There was a pause in which, knowing Jocelyn, I was expected to express my curiosity, perhaps even a touch of jealousy as well that she might have met someone new whom she might prefer to me, for I knew it had to be a man, otherwise she wouldn't have been so excited.

When I failed to reply, she hurried on.

'He's only just moved into the village so I thought I'd have a little party and introduce him to a few local people. You'll be there, won't you?'

So I said 'yes' because, in spite of everything, I'm quite fond of Jocelyn and I didn't want to be unkind to her. She's divorced, lonely and desperate for attention but there's no malice in her. Besides, I was a little curious. Although I try not to get too involved locally, there are certain social mores that have to be preserved if only for the sake of good manners and a quiet life. And for

5

Charlotte's sake as well. She, too, has to live in Northorpe, if only on a part-time basis.

'Yes. Fine. I'd love to come,' I told Jocelyn.

'Oh, that's marvellous! See you at eleven next Sunday!' she exclaimed so vivaciously that I began to regret having accepted.

So, at eleven o'clock yesterday, I got in the car and drove to Jocelyn's, which is on the far side of the village in a cul-de-sac of detached houses in the new development behind the school. There are half a dozen of them, built of brick with white-painted weather-boarding on the main gable which gives them a Scandinavian air, all the rage at the time they were put up in the Sixties.

There were only a few cars parked outside; most people would have walked. Three of them I recognised, but the fourth, a silver-grey Audi, was not one I knew and I assumed it belonged to the new arrival for whose sake Jocelyn was giving the party.

I could hear it as I got out of the car and walked down the flagged path to the back of the house: that convivial intermingling of voices, punctuated by laughter and higher-pitched exclamations, which is common to all gatherings of people in no matter what part of the world.

Seconds later, I had rounded the corner and there they all were, standing on Jocelyn's patio among her urns of pink geraniums and blue lobelia, and spilling over on to the lawn: the

6

cream of Northorpe society, relaxed and wearing the kind of smart, casual clothes that are *de rigueur* for get-togethers of this sort; the men in clean, well-ironed jeans or slacks worn with open-necked shirts, the younger women in the same sort of gear, although a few were a little more daring and sophisticated in skirts down to their ankles and blouses that had a touch of ethnicity about them.

Jocelyn was one of them, in a batik sarong and a short, tight-fitting top of dark red silk that allowed a glimpse of a sun-tanned midriff whenever she raised her arms.

Most of the guests were instantly recognisable: the Spensers; the Gowers; the Bensons; the tall, sandy-haired figure of Major Roth, pink-faced under a Panama hat, his hee-hawing laugh clearly audible above the general chatter; old Mrs Gunter holding court from a basket chair under the yellow and white striped sun umbrella; the Vicar, looking earnestly sociable, clutching a glass of white wine from which he took tiny, occasional sips as if from a communion chalice: the same crowd one could meet on a regular basis, if one wanted to, at dinner parties or bridge evenings, on Open days at one another's gardens or at fêtes to raise money for church repairs or the Conservative Party.

But there was one figure among them that was unfamiliar, although I could only see his back. It belonged to someone tall and dark-haired who was talking to the Hamiltons and Jocelyn and who was evidently being amusing for Sylvia Hamilton was laughing, her head thrown back.

It was probably the new arrival, I decided, and, as if on cue, Jocelyn looked across, saw me and, excusing herself from Sylvia and David, led the man towards me.

As I watched him approach, I recognised him immediately, not because I had seen him before but because of who he reminded me of.

It's absurd to say he's like M. M was shorter and stockier than this other man and much younger, with a flop of fair hair, like a schoolboy's, which fell over his forehead, and one of those ever-ready smiles that were switched on very quickly and crinkled up his eyes.

His *doppelgänger* is much taller and leaner, dark-haired and serious-looking, almost grave. He reminds me of photos of Arthur Miller as a young man. His smile is slow to come and seems more sincere than M's, but it has its own charm in the way it quirks up the right-hand corner of his mouth, which I suspect, like M's, is practised in front of a mirror. His mouth is his most attractive feature. The upper lip is long and thin, the lower one much fuller and curiously padded and dark-skinned, as if the blood is thicker there and much closer to the surface.

But the ethos of the man is very similar to

M's, if ethos is the right word to use. By this I mean his personality; his essence, if you like.

Jocelyn, who was still clutching him by the arm like a trophy she had just won, was smiling delightedly, her head on one side as she tried to read my reaction to him and to her intimacy with him.

What was she hoping for? A sign of jealousy? Or regret at her apparent loss to another man? Or perhaps my admiration? For she was looking superb with that glitter of sexual excitement about her which she hasn't worn for a long time.

'Alex, darling,' she was saying, 'I'd like you to meet Noel Murray. Noel, this is Alex Lambert, an old and very dear friend of mine.'

This hint of cause for sexual rivalry on his part appeared to fall on dead ground for he made no reaction to it as he held out his hand to me in a frank, open gesture that wasn't without a certain conscious charm.

'Delighted to meet you,' he said.

I made some reply, although my mind wasn't on this exchange of social pleasantries. I was thinking Noel Murray! His surname began with the same letter as M's. It was, of course, coincidental but, all the same, it seemed significant in some cock-eyed way.

Jocelyn was saying, 'Noel's renting that house just down the road from you so you'll be near neighbours.'

I was surprised by the information. The

Lawns is a modern, detached villa, too large I would have thought for a single man to occupy alone, and probably expensive. It had not long been on the market, the owners, a married couple with children, having put it up for rent a few weeks earlier when the husband's firm had sent him to Dubai on a year's transfer.

As if aware of my thoughts, or perhaps he was just very good at reading faces, Murray remarked, 'It's rather large for my needs but it's a useful base for looking around for somewhere more permanent. It's close to London as well.'

'You work in London?' I asked.

Again, he seemed anxious to put me right.

'Actually,' he said, and there was an apologetic, almost self-denigrating tone in his voice, 'I'm self-employed, so I work from home'.

'Oh, really?' I replied.

I refused to ask what he did and he apparently preferred not to tell me for he continued, turning the conversation away from himself, 'Jocelyn tells me you're an architect'.

'Yes, I am.'

My reply was deliberately short, not just because I dislike discussing what I do with strangers but also I was annoyed that Jocelyn had obviously spoken about me to him. I wondered what else she had told him; almost certainly that I had a profoundly deaf daughter. He was sensitive enough to pick up my reluctance and the conversation turned to the merits of village life. I can't remember exactly what was said but I was aware of a certain practised ease about him and his trick, for that was what I was sure it was, of giving his whole attention to the person he was talking to. Like the smile and the voice, I felt it was carefully cultivated and put on for the occasion as another man might use aftershave to enhance his image. It had the effect, of course, of flattering the person he was addressing so that he, or more often she, was made to feel the focus of all his attention and that no one else mattered.

After a few minutes, I made my excuses and went across the patio to join another group of people, the Bensons. I wanted to stand a little apart from Murray and observe him at work, so to speak. Jocelyn seemed disappointed I had moved away. I think she had wanted me to be impressed by Murray, her new conquest.

I was certainly curious about him and, as I chatted to the others, I watched him with covert attention. His success with women was immediately obvious. They loved his dark good looks, his social ease and pleasant manners, but mainly they fell for the way he focused on them. They glowed, those women. Even plain, middle-aged Phyliss Hardy opened up, like a flower emerging from a tight, green bud.

Jocelyn's reactions were also interesting.

She obviously resented Murray's attention being turned from her on to other women and, after two such encounters, she moved on alone to talk to some of the others, mostly the men and, in particular, those who were alone or had the least attractive wives.

I left soon afterwards, making a brief round of the guests to say goodbye, stopping last of all with Jocelyn, who lifted up her face for me to kiss her on both cheeks.

'Lovely party,' I told her. 'Thank you for asking me.'

She seemed downcast by my departure but brightened up at my remark and at the embrace, despite its conventionality.

As I paused at the gate leading off the patio to look back, one particular little tableau caught my attention and seemed significant.

It was of Murray talking to Mrs Gunter under her striped umbrella. He was bending down over her like a courtier waiting on the queen while she was looking coquettishly up at him, head on one side, rewarding him with a gracious smile as if she were conferring a knighthood on him. It was amusing yet at the same time oddly disturbing; quite why, I wasn't sure.

A few seconds later, he had moved away and Jocelyn, seizing her chance, immediately stepped forward to reclaim him, slipping her arm into his. His beam was now directed on to her as he took her hand, caressing the skin on the back of it with his thumb.

The smile she gave him was dazzling, like a flashbulb suddenly bursting into brilliance, making everything within its radius seem grey and lifeless in comparison.

Tuesday, 3rd June.
I've just reread the entry I wrote yesterday evening about Jocelyn and feel I haven't been very fair to her. I know I find her exasperating but now she's found Murray and the heat, so to speak, is turned on him rather than on me, I feel I can afford to be a little more generous towards her and less on the defensive. Before Murray's arrival, I was always having to fend her off. I'm a widower so I'm available; that's my trouble.

I could never have an affair with her. She's too needy. She demands constant attention and admiration, which I find exhausting after even an hour in her company. Physically she doesn't appeal to me either. She's too obvious; too colourful, with her auburn hair, her green iridescent eyelids, her deep pink lips and nails. She's also a disturbing mixture of surface self-confidence with a lot of insecurity underneath, which reminds me of the grass at the edge of a pond, lush and green and inviting, but, if you tread on it, you sink down into the black ooze below.

She draws attention to herself, laughing too much and flicking back her hair, or laying an

13

intimate hand on your arm when she talks to you. When she comes into a room, her eyes always search out any mirror hanging there and she flirts her head in its direction. It seems she needs to see her reflection in order to assure herself of her own reality. Without that image, she wouldn't exist. I'm aware of this when I see her with other people. They act as a kind of mirror for her and, if they ignore her or leave her out of the conversation, a light appears to go off inside her and her face seems to lack its usual definition. It's quite extraordinary to observe this transformation. Her flesh and skin seem to droop and her whole body sags as if someone has cut the little, invisible threads that hold her together. She looks like an abandoned child.

And yet, at the same time, there is something very admirable about her. She reminds me of a gallant little yacht, dressed overall with bunting, her paint- and brass-work gleaming, scudding along on the surface of life.

She was married to a wealthy businessman who owned, or so she told me one evening at the local pub when she had drunk too much and was boozily confidential, a whole string of boutiques in east London. She was the manageress of one of them, and they lived in a large house in Ilford. Her husband divorced his wife to marry her. Now, she admitted, with a little wry grimace, she was experiencing the same fate as that first wife. He traded her in, as they say, for a younger, trimmer model. But instead of dropping to pieces as some women might have done, she fought back, got awarded a substantial sum in alimony and moved down to Northorpe to be near her sister who lives in Witham. With the divorce settlement, she bought the house she's living in now and took out a lease on a dress shop in Chelmsford, which I gather is successful. But she needs a man. She is one of those women who is incomplete without one.

I'm genuinely concerned, though, about her and Murray, knowing from experience the kind of havoc a man like him can make of a woman's life. Despite the sophisticated veneer, underneath it she's naive and vulnerable, and too desperate to find herself another husband to realise what he's really like.

And I feel I *do* know what he's like, having made a study of M over the years. I've read books and articles about his type as well. He's what's known as a sociopath; the product of a personality disorder which displays certain anti-social characteristics, such as the incapacity to make lasting relationships or to empathise with someone else's pain. Sociopaths are often charming and fun to be with, but they are basically ruthless and manipulative and can be destructive, for they're out for whatever they can get for themselves, whether it's a financial, sexual or

15

professional advantage.

Because he's so like M, Murray fascinates me. I was too young when I first met M to recognise what he was although even at the age of eleven I knew there was something not quite right about him. I disliked and mistrusted him from instinct—his breezy manner, his way of ruffling my hair and treating me as if we were friends, his efforts to win me over by showing me simple conjuring tricks or kicking a ball about in the garden. I loathed his false *bonhomie*, even the smell of him: his aftershave and the odour of cigarettes on his clothes and hands. Young as I was, I saw through him, even though I didn't realise then what it was all leading up to.

I distrust and dislike Murray in the same way and my instincts tell me to steer well clear of him. But there is this awful fascination as well, which isn't going to be easy to throw off. I need to study him at close quarters as I did with M, only with an adult and objective eye. For I feel that, if I can understand M through Murray, I might be able to rid myself of the malign influence that M still seems to have over my life.

Friday, 6th June.

I was still thinking about M and Murray yesterday and, as a result, couldn't work on the design for that garage extension at Bellingdon. So, at six o'clock, having sat in front of the

16

plans on and off for most of the day and done virtually nothing, I decided to walk to Murray's house across the fields. It's almost half a mile by road, and probably a little further by the cross-country route as you have to make quite a wide detour round the grounds of Northorpe Hall.

Approaching Murray's house from the rear gave me an unfamiliar view of the place as I normally drive past it and, if I bother to look at it at all, I catch only a glimpse of it between the trees. Seeing it on foot and from the end of the back garden, I could see much more detail.

Like its name, The Lawns, it's a pretentious place, a Sixties house pretending to be eighteenth century; all white-painted stucco and sash windows with a Georgian-style conservatory tacked on one end. It even has half-pilasters and triangular pediments above the main windows. But for all this attention to detail, there's something about its design that's fundamentally bogus. The proportions are wrong and give the impression of an oblong box of a house on to which over-large embellishments have been added in order to give it a gracious, period style but which ends up looking ridiculous.

The lawns after which the house was presumably named have the same absurd pretensions. In the first place, there's only one lawn which was supposed, I imagine, to ape the long stretches of grass behind a country

17

house sweeping down to a lake, affording glimpses of statues placed among the trees and ornamental shrubs. In reality, it's about the size of a tennis court, broken in the centre by one of those pre-formed plastic pools one can buy at garden centres, with a fountain in the shape of a dolphin squirting small jets of water into the air.

I kept well out of sight of the house for Murray was at home. At least, I could see his car parked at the side of the house. There was no sign of him though. After spending about ten minutes watching the place, I moved away and set off to walk home across the fields. But Murray's pseudo-Georgian house had reminded me of the real eighteenth-century mansion, Northorpe Hall, and I decided to stop there on the way back to take the taste, so to speak, of The Lawns out of my mouth.

There's not much left of the house itself. It was gutted by fire in the 1920s and a large part of the ruins were demolished because they were considered unsafe. All that remains of it now are a few brick walls, stripped of their stucco, some of them containing fireplace and window openings. There are also rows of horizontal slots, which once held the joists that supported the upper floors. There are one or two other relics as well. Some of the flagstones of the original terrace are still in place, as well as the three steps that used to lead up to the garden entrance, which is now nothing more than a large, rectangular hole.

Grass and ivy have taken over the site but, if you look carefully, you can find other remnants of the original building scattered around. I've found fragments of black and white mosaic tiles just inside the doorway opening, all that remains of the original flooring of the main hall and, hidden under the clumps of nettles and the wild buddleias, the seeds of which must have blown there from the cultivated bushes in the shrubbery, there are broken pieces of ornamental stone, some quite elaborately carved, along with countless shards of glass from the tiers of sash windows that once looked out over the garden.

I know what it used to look like because, not long after I moved into the village, I came across the ruin when I was out walking and fell in love with it. As a result, I've spent hours researching its background in the archives in Colchester. Its history goes back to the time of Henry VIII, during the Reformation and the dissolution of the monasteries when land belonging to the Catholic church was either sold or given away to Henry's cronies.

One of the lucky ones was Sir William Oxleigh, who was awarded with a parcel of church land in Northorpe, on which he built a small manor house where he lived with his family and farmed his acres. The house and land remained with the Oxleigh family until the beginning of the eighteenth century, when the then owner went bankrupt and the estate was sold to George Withers, a wealthy corn dealer with aspirations of becoming a squire. It was his son, Henry, who demolished the original Tudor manor house and built in its place the present Northorpe Hall, or what is left of it, using all the fashionable architectural techniques of the time, including the tall, elegant sash windows, the imposing pillared porticos at the front and rear of the house, a terrace with a stone balustrade and a double set of steps sweeping up to the garden entrance.

The interior was no less splendid. The rooms were decorated with elaborate plaster cornices, carved doorcases and fireplaces. I once discovered part of a cherub's head among the debris, its curls still more or less intact but only a fragment of a wing and one plump shoulder remaining. According to the photographs of the interior taken in the 1890s and preserved among the archives, it was part of the mantelpiece in the drawing room, which had been particularly lavishly decorated with swags of roses and ivy leaves, held up at the corners by two winged cherubs.

Those photographs were a godsend for they enabled me to reconstruct the house in my imagination and, what was more important, the garden, which, like the house, lay in ruins. It is considerably smaller than the original grounds for, over the years, much of the estate had been sold. The first to go was the farmland, auctioned off acre by acre until nothing was left by the end of the nineteenth century except for a couple of paddocks and a hayfield. The First World War put an end to these and to much of the remainder. The local men who had looked after the grounds were called up and were either killed in the trenches or, if they survived the slaughter, preferred not to return to the low-paid menial work on the gardens, opting instead for factory work in Chelmsford or London.

It was then that much of the garden was sold until all that was left was the area immediately behind the house consisting mainly of lawn and flower borders, and about a quarter of an acre of shrubbery, known as the Dell. This was probably preserved because it contained some interesting relics of the original eighteenth-century pleasure gardens, through which the Withers family and their guests could stroll after luncheon and, turning a corner, come across a carefully positioned piece of statuary or a rustic bench or, most fashionable of all, a folly in the form of ruined Greek temple; fake, of course.

Most of those features have long disappeared but two remain: a stone Sphinx squatting among some overgrown rhododendrons, only its head poking through the leaves, its features blotched green and brown with lichen; and an artificial grotto built of huge rocks that must have cost a small fortune to transport to the site. They have been constructed into a semi-circular wall about seven feet high, the sides coming round to form two wings which turn the interior space into a small amphitheatre, decorated with shells set into patterns, many of which have, over the years, dropped out of their settings. The whole is roofed with stone slabs and the front wall has been built up to form two arched and pillared window openings, Gothic in design, and a central doorway, also arched and pillared.

Because they may have been considered a danger, the window embrasures have been closed off with strong, vertical iron bars and, in the case of the doorway, with an iron gate that covers the whole opening. All these fixtures have gone rusty with age and the original lock on the gate has been broken so that it can be easily swung open.

I often walk over to Northorpe Hall and sit in the grotto on one of the semi-circular stone benches that are fixed to the back wall. It is a peaceful place, the silence broken only by the songs of birds in the garden and the patter of water-drops falling down the back wall, where a natural spring has been rechannelled to trickle over the rocks and fall into a shell-shaped bowl held out by the statue of a young girl, dressed in Grecian robes, which stands beside it. From the bowl, the water overflows into a small pool at her feet, lined with shells and pebbles, from where it drains away into the ground.

The statue, half lifesize, is, I assume, of some water nymph. Frost and time and the accretions of green slime have eaten into the surface of the marble, leaving it stained and pitted. Even so, it's still possible to make out some of the details of the figure, the folds in the drapes, for example, and the coronet of flowers she wears on her hair. Her features also are blurred but something of her original beauty has remained in the curve of her forehead, the delicate arms and her gentle smile. She reminds me of Charlotte, especially in the tilt of her head, a pose Charlotte often assumes when she is concentrating on reading someone's lips, as if the words so formed might become audible if she watches intently enough.

It is easy to get into the garden. At the front of the house, an eight-foot high, chain-link fence cuts off access from the road and a notice warning that Trespassers will be Prosecuted has been fixed to the padlocked gates. But at the back the security isn't so tight and in one place there is a gap in the fence where the metal supports have become dislodged and a section of the wire meshing has collapsed almost to the ground, so, apart from the undergrowth of holly and bramble bushes, there is nothing to deter the determined trespasser.

Over the years I've been coming here, I've established my own entrance and exit through this gap by the simple method of pushing myself in backwards through the bushes, shielding my face with my arms.

On my way home yesterday, I went first to the house, cutting across what had once been a lawn but which is now a rough field of meadow grass and wild flowers, some of which I recognised from botany lessons at school, among them speedwell and clover and ox-eye daisies.

It was what Charlotte and I call a Wordsworth evening—very still, not a leaf or a blade of grass stirring; the 'holy time, quiet as a nun, breathless with adoration'. It's a line I've never felt entirely comfortable with. It's OTT in its conscious straining after poetic effect. All the same, there is a certain truth about it. When the air is hushed and the light has a gentle, serene quality about it, there is a special tranquillity that reminds me of an empty church holding its breath, as if waiting for something miraculous to happen.

I entered the ruins across the terrace, mounting the three steps that once led to the garden entrance. I know the lay-out of the place from the old photographs and architect's plans I'd found in the archives. To the left was where the dining room had once been, with the library behind it; and to the right the drawing room where the magnificent mantelpiece of roses and cherubs had once formed the centrepiece; gone, now, of course, although the fireplace opening is still there in the wall, its brick lining still bearing the blackened soot-stains from the fires that had once burned there.

It is these relics of the lives of the people who once occupied this ruined building that fascinate me so much and draw me back to the place time and time again. It is like hearing a voice from the past. They rouse in me a gentle melancholy which I find oddly soothing.

When my mother ran away with M, my father sent me to a boarding school for clergymen's sons in Suffolk, where there were the ruins of a church on the outskirts of the nearby village. In the turmoil of emotions I felt after she abandoned us, which at times threatened to engulf me, I used to cycle over to this church and sit on the grass inside the roofless nave, looking at the branches of the trees framed in the arch of the east window with its broken mullions. There I would find a temporary peace before going back to the unfamiliar noise and restlessness of the school, where silence and solitude, even in chapel, were impossible to attain.

On the way home, I stopped, as I always do, at the grotto. Unlike the house, it holds no intimations of the past, only the present, and of Charlotte, embodied in the statue of the nymph holding out her marble dish to catch the water-drops. I caught some of the water in my own cupped hands and drank it, another ritual that is a relic of the superstitions of childhood, like wishing on a new moon or avoiding the cracks in the paving stones as I walked. I used to think that if I performed these acts punctiliously, then my mother would come home. In the same way, if I drink a little water from the grotto, then Charlotte will be safe and well. I'm not so stupid to hope that she might one day gain her hearing.

It's ridiculous, of course. I realise this myself. But once the ritual had been established, I daren't break it in case it brings bad luck; another absurdity.

So as I sipped the water, which tasted of leaf-mould, I thought of her instead of M and my mother. I shall be seeing Charlotte this coming weekend. Sitting on one of the stone benches, I planned what we'd do over those two days. Go swimming perhaps. Or to the cinema. Or drive over to Maldon and watch the boats on the river; perhaps even hire one and go rowing.

I want every weekend we spend together to be special. So when I walked home, my mind was full of Charlotte, not M or Murray, and I felt at peace.

Tuesday, 10th June.
Evening. As I can't phone her, I've just

written to Charlotte part of my long, twice-weekly 'diary' letters, as I call them, telling her everything I've done since last Friday, the day the previous letter was posted. When I wrote 'everything', I realised it was not true; it was one of those evasions that are not exactly lies but are certainly not the whole truth. So when I described Jocelyn's party, I made no mention of Murray, an omission I can explain only to myself. Charlotte knows nothing about my mother and M, only that she died when I was still at school. I would no more write to Charlotte about M, or Murray, come to that, than I would consciously expose her to some dangerous contagion, like smallpox or cholera.

Of course, I didn't mention my visit to Murray's house. I simply wrote that I went for a walk across the fields. And, oddly enough, I left out the visit to Northorpe Hall, quite why, I'm not sure myself. Charlotte knows about the ruins and once said she'd like to see them, but I told her they were private property so we'd be trespassing if we went there. I also made the excuse they were dangerous; parts of the walls were likely to fall down and the ground is so overgrown that one could easily trip over branches and pieces of fallen masonry.

All of this is quite true, but I know this isn't the real reason for not taking her there. I'm not sure myself what that is—at least, not completely. It's connected with M and those other ruins I used to visit when I was at school in Suffolk, but I can't, or rather won't, examine the memories in any detail. There is too much pain associated with them. Shame, as well. And guilt. I still can't bear to face them full on or allow Charlotte to be associated with them in any way. I feel they would besmirch her or, if not her, then our relationship. It would be like rubbing one's fingers over a peach and destroying its bloom.

Sunday, 15th June. 10.30 p.m.
Charlotte came on Friday evening. As usual, Pauline Bradshaw collected her and her own daughter, Fiona, from Hillside after school and took them back to their house for an hour to let the two girls have time together. Like Charlotte, Fiona is a weekly boarder at Hillside, but she comes home every weekend. Charlotte used to do the same but this year a peripatetic art teacher started taking a group of the older girls out for a sketching class, which Charlotte was keen to join. So I agreed although I miss her not being here on those weekends.

When she is, I share the driving of the two girls to and from the school with the Bradshaws; one of them, usually Pauline, picking them up at Hillside on Friday afternoons, while I take them back on Sundays in readiness for school again on Monday mornings.

I have a lot in common with the Bradshaws.

Like me, they gave up their old life and moved to Foxton so that Fiona could go to school at Hillside. Derek Bradshaw used to work for a publicity agency in London and would, I imagine, have had quite a secure, well-paid position there. Instead, he's started up a small one-man printing firm in Dewsbury, a couple of miles from Banfield, where the school is. He does headed writing paper, circulars, advertising leaflets; that sort of thing. In fact, I got him to do all the advertising for me when I first moved here. Pauline Bradshaw helps out by manning the phone when he's out of the office for any length of time, delivering orders or seeing a customer. She also does most of the paperwork at home.

I like her. She's very pleasant and unpretentious. I'm not so sure about him. He's all right, I suppose, but he's not as friendly as she is. I think he found giving up his job and becoming self-employed rather stressful. He doesn't much care for living in the country either. He's always busy and seems to have no time for anything but work.

I've asked them several times to come over here for a meal but he's usually got some excuse not to come. If he does, he's very heavy going; not much fun as a dinner guest.

Although Fiona is a year younger than Charlotte, I'm delighted the two girls are friends. She needs that close contact with someone of her own age. I'm a bit uneasy, though, over her insistence that she catches the bus back from the Bradshaws' on Friday afternoons, rather than letting me pick her up or one or other of the Bradshaws drive her home, although both Derek and Pauline are willing to do so should it rain, for example, or if some other minor crisis occurred. I can understand Charlotte's feelings about wanting to have this independence. She's fourteen now and doesn't want to be treated like a child any more. As she pointed out, the journey is straightforward. She catches the bus almost outside the Bradshaws' house and it comes directly to Northorpe; no changing. She gets off just down the road from here, a distance of about fifty yards. She can pronounce Northorpe fairly clearly, but in case she finds any difficulty in buying a ticket, I always make sure she's got exactly the right fare on the Sundays before I drop her and Fiona off at school. I realise she's growing up and that at some point she'll have to make her own way in the world. I can't go on protecting her for ever.

We had a wonderful weekend together. We lazed about on Saturday morning and I took her swimming in the afternoon. On Sunday morning we drove over to the garden centre at Church End to choose roses for planting in the back garden in the autumn. That's Charlotte's idea. She thinks the garden is too dull and conventional with just the lawn and shrubs planted along the sides. She's designed two

30

semi-circular beds, backed with trellis and planted with roses; bush roses in the front, underplanted with bulbs, and climbing roses at the back to cover the trellis. She's taken so much trouble over the plan, measuring it out and making a watercolour sketch of the finished effect that I don't like to point out that it will take a hell of a lot of work to lay it out, not to mention the spraying and pruning that will follow. As it is now, I can whizz up and down the lawn in half an hour with the motor mower. But I can't bear to disappoint her. As we discussed her idea, I wondered if garden design might be a possible career for her. It's worth bearing in mind and making enquiries about what qualifications and training she might need after she's left school. It also occurred to me that we might go into partnership together, with me planning the building of a house, say, and her designing the layout of the garden.

Friday, 20th June.
I'm not sure if I've done the right thing. I acted completely on impulse, which is often a bad idea, as I've discovered from experience.

Anyway, I had to go into the village to post some letters and I decided to walk there instead of taking the car. Jocelyn Harvey was coming out of the shop just as I was putting the letters into the post-box. Of course, I had to stop and talk to her. In fact, I felt a little

31

guilty as I haven't seen or spoken to her since her party a couple of weeks ago.

She was aware of this herself because as we met she said, with mock severity, 'Hello, Alex. Goodness, you're quite a stranger!'

She was looking particularly dashing in a pair of blue denim jeans and a bright pink checked shirt, worn loose, and I suddenly felt very warm towards her and said, on the spur of the moment, 'If you're free tomorrow about twelve, do come round for a drink'.

I realised it was a mistake as soon as I said it.

She smiled coquettishly, tilting her head to one side.

'Oh, Alex, I'd love to!' she exclaimed, and then added, her voice rising to a mock wail, 'But I'm afraid I can't! I've promised Noel I'd meet him at the Feathers for lunch. What a shame!'

I could have shrugged and smiled and said, 'Oh, well. Perhaps another time,' and left it at that. But the mention of Murray's name acted as a kind of challenge. I haven't seen him since Jocelyn's party and really haven't thought about him much; Charlotte's visit and the planning of the rose garden having taken up any free time and interest. But, suddenly reminded of him, it seemed a good opportunity to observe him at close quarters in Jocelyn's company, so that I might see exactly how he goes about the business of seduction and perhaps learn from it a little of how M must have operated.

So I said, 'Why don't you both come round? It'll have to be a snack lunch, I'm afraid. Say at twelve o'clock?'

'Oh, Alex, I'd love to!' Jocelyn cried. 'And so will Noel. Only the other day he mentioned you. He said how much he'd enjoyed talking to you at my party. So I know he'll come like a shot.'

I refused to be flattered by Jocelyn's remarks for I guessed they were said less for my benefit than to show me that she and Murray were on fairly intimate terms, a not very subtle way of trying to rouse my jealousy, which it failed to do. I felt only relief that her attention was taken off me and transferred to Murray. All the same, I felt a twinge of concern on her behalf. If, as I suspect, she's looking for a secure and lasting relationship, I doubt very much if Murray can supply it. Even so, it will be interesting to see the pair of them together tomorrow lunchtime.

Saturday, 21st June. Evening.

The lunch was interesting. Jocelyn had dressed herself up as if for a cocktail party in a low-cut blouse, ankle-length skirt and lots of costume jewellery. Murray was in much better taste, very down-beat and casual in jeans and a T-shirt, but still managing to look expensive and fashionable. Much as I dislike the man, I have to admit he has style.

Jocelyn was on a high. With two men apparently vying for her favours, she sparkled as brightly as her earrings and the gold chains round her neck, playing the coquette with both of us.

I found her vivacity intensely wearying and I think Murray did as well. At one point during the lunch, her trick of putting one hand on his arm and laughing sideways into his face became obviously embarrassing to him and he shifted his chair slightly so that he was out of reach of her and put on his sunglasses as a further deterrent.

She was sensitive enough to be aware of the meaning behind his actions and to be hurt by it. From then on, she lost some of her sparkle. I felt a little sorry for her but relieved that the conversation, which up to then had been largely directed by her and was full of innuendos and attempts to angle for compliments, passed on to other topics.

I was keen to find out more about him but very anxious not to show my hand, so I began with general questions: How did he like the village? Had he settled into the house? Had he joined any of the local clubs: the historical society, the bridge club?

He seemed frank in his answers but, in fact, gave very little away. Yes, he liked the village. It was very convenient being near to Chelmsford for getting the train up to London.

Yes, the house was fine; a little too big perhaps, but he liked the feeling of space. Societies? Well, it was a bit early yet. He was still feeling his way into the community and, anyway, he wasn't much of a joiner.

He became more evasive when I asked about his background. Although his answers appeared to be candid, his body language subtly altered. His hands, which had been lying loosely on top of the table, tightened and he held his head slightly averted so that he wasn't looking directly at me. Because of the sunglasses he was wearing, I couldn't read his eyes.

Where had he lived before? London. In fact, that was why he'd moved out to the country. London had become so noisy and expensive that he felt he needed a change.

At this point, Jocelyn broke in.

'Oh, how could you bear to leave London?' she exclaimed. 'All those wonderful shops and restaurants!'

He looked amused.

'But you can't go shopping or dining out every moment of the day,' he replied. 'It's those other times when you grow to dislike it— the crowds, the litter everywhere, the traffic. I was glad to get out of it.'

The last remark had a note of genuine repugnance about it and I wondered if his dislike was not so much for the place as for some other aspect of it. Had something happened there that had caused this aversion? Or was it a person he'd met there?

I wasn't given the chance to follow this up because he abruptly but pleasantly changed the subject.

'Tell me about yourself,' he said, taking off the sunglasses and looking directly at me. 'How long have you been living in Northorpe?'

'About nine years.'

'So you're part of the village now?'

Jocelyn intervened again with a bright laugh.

'Oh, God, Noel! You really are an innocent when it comes to village life! You have to live here for yonks before you're fully accepted, especially by the real villagers, the ones who were born here. All the rest of us are newcomers. I always say you have to give at least a good dozen dinner parties before you're accepted by the local establishment; unless, of course, you can buy your way in like the Buchanans did or Mrs Gunter.'

'How fascinating! How did they manage that?' Murray asked, turning his attention fully on her like a searchlight. He seemed genuinely interested and amused by what she had to say, a characteristic that I had noticed before as being part of his charisma. It was intensely flattering and many people, men as well as women, young and old, would respond to this attention, particularly the lonely and vulnerable. I remembered that occasion at

Jocelyn's party when he had squatted on his heels in front of old Mrs Gunter, and her pleasure at being courted by this good-looking stranger.

I realised a little belatedly that he had tried the same trick on me a little earlier when he had started to ask me about myself, although he was probably motivated by the need to switch my attention away from himself for whatever reason. Realising this, I suddenly felt strangely excited and stimulated. Here was someone who was a great deal more complex and subtle than anyone else I had ever known; more so than M. I'd been too young at the time I'd met M to appreciate fully the extent of his deviousness. Nevertheless, even M didn't come up to Murray's standard.

I made up my mind there and then to get to know him better by meeting him when Jocelyn wasn't around, so that I could concentrate on him exclusively and, by using some of his own techniques, to probe a little deeper below that charming, relaxed exterior and try to find his particular weakness, because I'm sure under the surface he's as vulnerable as the rest of us.

Later, towards the end of the lunch, I was given an opening to further contact with him when he happened to mention Northorpe Hall and asked if I knew anything about it. Loath though I was to encourage him to visit the ruins that I look on as my own special place, I gave him a brief account of it, leaving out any mention of the grotto. If he found it, so be it. But I certainly wasn't going to point him in its direction. I offered to lend him my folder of archive material, which I'd photocopied from the original documents, making a silent proviso that I'd go through it first and remove any references to the grotto, including the photograph of it. He seemed eager to see the folder and, to prevent him from asking to borrow it there and then, I said I'd look it out and give him a call when I'd found it. In exchange, he went out to his car to get one of his business cards, which he handed to me.

Like him, it was in excellent taste: no mock Gothic or italic script but a plain Gill font on an oblong of good quality cream-coloured card, which simply gave his name, his address and his phone and fax numbers, as well as is email address. Discreetly placed below this information were the words 'Financial Consultant'.

As I read it, it struck me that I might find out more about him and his background by putting myself forward as a possible client. That way, he might tell me where he'd practised in London and why exactly he'd left there. It seemed to me highly unusual that someone of his profession should move out of London, one of the great investment capitals of the world, to an Essex village.

Wednesday, 25th June. Evening.
I waited until yesterday before telephoning Murray and suggesting I drop the Northorpe Hall folder at his house tomorrow afternoon, with the excuse that I'd be passing it on the way back from seeing a client at Nettleden, which was true. It also served as an excuse for not inviting him here to pick it up. I wanted to see him in his own habitat, so to speak.

I got there at four o'clock as arranged and was shown by Murray into what I assume was the drawing room; a hideously pretentious room full of leather sofas and club chairs, fake antiques and gold-framed reproductions of Constable landscapes of the type that can be bought in the furnishing departments of certain large London stores and probably cost a small fortune. The fitted carpet was dusky pink and matched the curtains, which were heavily swagged and trimmed with gold fringing three inches deep.

Although I kept my expression bland, Murray anticipated my reaction and said with amusement, 'Dreadful, isn't it? To misquote Kenny Everett, it's in the worst possible taste. But it was the only furnished place I could find at short notice. Do sit down. Would you like a drink?'

'No thanks,' I replied, lowering myself into one of the leather sofas, which subsided voluptuously like soft flesh as I sank down into

39

it. 'I've got a lot of work to do when I get home. I'll need a clear head.'

He nodded in agreement, one self-employed businessman appreciating the restraints imposed on another, and I thought how quickly he'd established contact with me. It was smart work on his part and I had to admire the speed with which he had demonstrated that we were two of a kind over the matter of taste and professional conduct. At the same time, I wondered why he wanted to get to know me and what he hoped to get out of it, for I was under no illusions that Murray was acting entirely out of self-interest.

I handed the file over to him and he thanked me with what seemed like genuine gratitude, opening it up and taking an eager glance at its contents.

'This is marvellous, Alex!' he exclaimed. 'You don't mind me calling you Alex, do you? And please do call me Noel.' And here he glanced towards me with a quick, sincere smile that crinkled up the corners of his eyes and reminded me so vividly of M that I wanted to get up and walk out of the room. But all I could do was nod in agreement, although I refused to speak to him to acknowledge this imposed intimacy.

He seemed unaware of any animosity on my part. Head bent over the folder, he was busy turning the pages and commenting on their contents.

'Wonderful photographs!' he remarked. 'They really capture that Edwardian period. Look at the number of servants they had! And the clothes, especially the women's! God, they must have been impossibly hot in the summer.'

He spoke in this manner for several minutes in an easy conversational style, commenting on the same features that I myself had noticed when I had first seen the photographs—the overfurnished rooms, the elaborate decorations, the extensive gardens. He was even perceptive enough to notice the empty space on one of the pages where I'd removed the photocopy of the one of the grotto from behind its transparent, protective covering sheet.

'What should be there?' he asked.

I got up to look more closely as if I had no idea what was missing.

'Oh, that!' I said dismissively. 'It was a shot of the garden but the photocopy was very dark. I decided not to use it.'

He seemed to accept the explanation, although he went on looking at that page, which contained views of the flowerbeds, for several more moments before asking, 'Can you get into the grounds? I've noticed the security fence in the front and from there you can't see much of what's left of the house because of the trees and the bushes.'

I lied quite shamelessly without even thinking about it, motivated by an overwhelming desire not to have him poking about the ruins and, in particular, finding the grotto. It was mine and he had no right to go there.

'No, I'm afraid you can't,' I replied. 'The whole site's fenced off and I would've thought it'd be a dangerous place to explore. It's all very overgrown, almost impenetrable. If you fell and broke your leg in there it might be months before anyone found you.'

'Ah, well. Never mind,' he said with a shrug. 'But may I keep the folder for a little longer? I'd like to study it in more detail.'

'Of course,' I said. I had no hesitation about agreeing to that. It would give me a point of further contact with him for I was still curious to find out why he was so intent on cultivating an acquaintance with me, convinced there had to be an ulterior motive.

He was saying, 'I can understand your interest in the place. As an architect, you must find the plans and drawings alone intriguing. And speaking of architecture, you mentioned on the phone that you were seeing a client this afternoon. I hope the meeting went well?'

I was relieved the conversation had turned away from Northorpe Hall and, with more enthusiasm than I might have shown under other circumstances, I replied, 'Yes, it did as a matter of fact. Thank you for asking'.

'May I ask what it was for?'

I said with deliberate deprecation, 'Oh, just

a house extension out at Nettleden; nothing more exciting, I'm afraid, than an extra garage with a fourth bedroom over it. Not a new cathedral, I'm sorry to say; not even a supermarket.'

He was silent for a moment and then said, 'May I be even more curious and ask you if you found it difficult to set up here as a self-employed professional? How did you go about it in the first place? Did you advertise?'

I wondered if this was the motive behind his interest in me—simply a desire to pick my brains and make use of my experience.

'Yes, I put adverts in the local papers,' I told him. 'And in the *Yellow Pages*. If you're thinking of doing the same, it's worth paying a little extra to get one of those bigger display adverts with an illustration. They're much more likely to be noticed. If you're interested, I could put you in touch with someone who'd design one for you.'

I was thinking of Derek Bradshaw, who would appreciate any business that came his way.

'Thanks for the offer. I may take you up on that,' he replied and went on to ask after a moment's pause, 'Have you always been self-employed?'

I hesitated, not wanting to give too much away to this man, but I was aware I'd asked him similar questions when we'd first met at Jocelyn's, a state of affairs I felt sure he remembered, too, and which he was making use of for his own benefit.

'No; I used to be a partner in a firm.'

'In London?'

'In Manchester.'

He seemed taken aback by this.

'Manchester? Why on earth did you come down here?'

I knew I mustn't give him the real reasons— the death of my wife and the need to find a good school for Charlotte, who was then nearly five. The decision wasn't really mine. It was made for me by the discovery that one of the best private schools for the deaf was at Banfield in Essex, where she could be a weekly boarder. The sale of my house in Manchester and my partnership had largely paid for the move, the purchase of the house in Northorpe and had also financed me for the first two years until I had established myself as a self-employed architect, working from home. This meant I was there whenever Charlotte needed me, not just at weekends. I could not bear to repeat my own experiences as a child when, after my own mother's defection, I had been bundled away to that boarding school in Suffolk at the age of ten to come home only during the holidays, not even at half-terms and weekends.

Murray, who had been watching my face closely, was aware he was treading on sensitive ground and had the good manners to withdraw immediately.

'I'm so sorry. I'm obviously prying. Do forgive me.'

The apology was charmingly made and apparently sincere, so why did I feel so defenceless? Murray could not have known my own vulnerability, which left me open to attack. It was paranoia, I knew. I had no reason to suspect that he'd found out about Charlotte or the fact that my mother had abandoned me for a man very like himself. But I couldn't help feeling that we were like two swordsmen, circling round each other as we waited for the other to lower his guard momentarily so that the *coup de grâce* could be delivered.

Much as I longed to get away from the man, I stayed for another five minutes, fearing that, if I left immediately, he would realise just how disturbed I had been by his questions. I had no intention of letting him think he had an advantage over me. So I sat there, smiling and exchanging pleasantries. Did he play golf? There was a good course at Hambledon only a couple of miles away. And the leisure centre at the Tudor Garden hotel, also at Hambledon, was open to non-residents, although the membership fees were rather pricey.

At last, I thought it time to go so I made my excuses and got to my feet. Murray escorted me to the door, thanking me again for letting him browse through the Northorpe Hall file. If it was all right by me, he'd like to keep it for a week or so and return it later.

The perfect host, he stood under the ridiculously over-sized pillared portico to see me off, raising a hand in salute as I turned out of the drive.

I haven't been able to settle since that encounter with him. I came home and did some work on the plans for the barn conversion at Thurston for the Newells, a project that normally would have excited me. It's a beautiful seventeenth-century building of beams in-filled with lath and plaster which, with a little care and imagination, can be converted into a four-bedroomed house without ruining the original structure. I see it as a wonderful challenge but I couldn't settle. Instead, I started marking out the new rose-beds from the plan Charlotte drew up last weekend.

Two a.m.

I slept so badly I eventually gave up and came downstairs for a whisky and soda. I had this dream, which I can't properly remember except that it was to do with M and also with Murray, who were somehow fused together into one individual. I was walking through a wood following this M/Murray figure, which I couldn't see although I felt its presence very strongly. I thought at first that the wood was the one at Northorpe Hall and that I was remembering it from my walk there the other day. Strange how in some dreams the rational part of one's mind remains awake and one can still think logically. I realised in the dream that it was not the same wood but an entirely different one which for some reason was dangerous to enter. I was just about to recognise and name it when I suddenly awoke with that lurch back into consciousness that leaves one's heart banging like a drum. I used to wake like that as a child, experiencing that same dreadful panic of finding myself alone in the dark, not knowing where I was or what had frightened me.

Damn Murray! And damn M! Their dual personality still hangs about me even in broad daylight.

Thursday, 26th June.

I still haven't been able to shake off Murray and M. They still haunt my thoughts and have become so intimately fused together that they have become one single identity, so that I can no longer summon them up individually. It's absurd that when I think of Murray I see M and vice versa.

It seemed the only sensible solution was to remind myself of M's image, so I've spent most of this morning searching out the box of old photographs that I know is somewhere in the house. Before I moved here from Manchester, I chucked away a lot of stuff I wouldn't need again, mostly papers, letters and such like. Some, of course, I kept; letters from my mother and my wife, which she sent before we were married, as well as some of the photographs. Those I kept back I put into a box file, which I brought with me to Northorpe. I know there's a photo of M among them because I remember hesitating over whether or not to throw it away and then, suddenly making up my mind, I shoved it into the file along with the other mementoes. Why I kept it, I don't know. Perhaps for such as this present eventuality when I might need to be reminded of him. Sometimes one's own motives are as impenetrable as a stranger's.

Whatever my own reasons might have been, I only know my need to find that photograph of M was far stronger than my desire to work on the Thurston barn conversion. So I spent a good two hours searching for the box, which I found eventually in a cupboard at the very back of the attic and, although I couldn't remember putting it there, I think I understand why I chose that particular dark corner. It was the out-of-sight-out-of-mind principle.

It was covered with dust, which I wiped away with a wad of paper handkerchiefs before carrying it downstairs to my office, where I shoved aside the plans I'd been working on to make room for it. There were more photographs in it than I remembered, held together by a large rubber band that had perished so that the bundle slithered apart as I picked it up. Shuffling them together, I looked at them individually, laying aside those I didn't want in a separate pile. Out of those that were left, I kept a few to study more closely.

There is something particularly poignant about old photographs, especially those of people who are now dead. Sometimes these are the only mementoes of them: fading images, mostly in black and white, of faces caught in a split second of time and transferred on to an oblong of paper, which probably also preserves other relics of these long-dead identities that are even more insubstantial—their fingerprints.

So does the snapshot of my mother taken in the vicarage garden years ago, wearing a polka dot dress and holding me in her arms swathed in a long shawl, bear the imprint of her fingers as she took the photograph out of the packet to examine it when it came back from the developer's?

There are several other photographs of her and I study each in turn, particularly those taken not long before her death. These images disturbed me more than I'd expected for, although I'm familiar with them, it's several years since I last looked at them. Since then I've made a conscious effort not to recall her so that even my memories of her have faded like the photos I'd put into the box file and hidden in the attic. Looking at them again after so long an interval, it is a shock to be reminded how beautiful she was and how like Charlotte. They both have the same thick, light-brown hair, which is almost blonde, and that direct gaze that can be disconcertingly candid. As far as I can remember, her eyes were also blue but not, I think, quite that same startling colour as Charlotte's; the bright, clear blue of certain flowers. The nearest comparison I can make is with speedwell flowers, which have that same brilliance.

But it's not my mother's physical features I remember most clearly but her presence, which is as elusive as a perfume or a chord of music heard from a distance, echoes of the senses that can never be precisely analysed and which words barely describe. Her laughter. Her gaiety. Her lightness of movement. Her sudden impulses, like the time I came on her unexpectedly in the garden and saw her tossing armfuls of fallen leaves up into the air and laughing like a child as they fluttered down about her.

None of the photographs of her capture this quicksilver quality of hers. How could they? The posed images present her in a quite different role—the vicar's wife, the mother, the member of all those committees and societies on which she was expected to serve.

My memories of my father are clearer. He was upright, straightforward, a man of honour and rectitude, a man of God. That is immediately apparent in his photographs. In all of them he is wearing his dog-collar, often his cassock. Like a soldier, he is never off-duty. He stands four-square, shoulders back, feet slightly apart, his hands clasped in front of him, as if taking part in an ecclesiastic parade.

Why did they ever marry?

Seen from my point of view as an adult, I'm only too clearly aware of their incompatibility and it puzzles me why two such intelligent people couldn't see it for themselves, although, in the case of my father, I can understand why he fell in love with my mother. She was young, pretty, warm, affectionate, and it was as a man, not as a man of God, that he chose her. As for her, I have no idea. Perhaps she felt safe with him. He was several years older, already established in his career, a rock to cling to. Oddly enough, his name was Peter, which means a rock, and it was the name he chose for me at my christening, only I haven't used it for years, preferring my second name, Alexander, named after his father. The first, Peter, brings with it too much emotional baggage and, as soon as I left home, I discarded it along with those other beliefs he tried so hard to hand on to me.

I understand her father, whose name I don't know, was an alcoholic. It was one of the few details my father told me about my mother's family, and only as a kind of awful warning of the perils of drink when, as a student home for the vacation, I used to slip along to the local pub for an occasional pint. The only other fact I knew about her background, which she herself told me, was that her grandmother was born deaf, and that inheritance I haven't been able to discard.

Given all this, it seems inevitable to me now that their marriage was bound to fail. She craved warmth and love and laughter, which he couldn't give her, as well as sexual satisfaction. Looking back, I have no doubt about that last need although as a child it never crossed my mind. And all of these longings M satisfied, if only on a temporary basis.

I shuffled quickly through the last photographs until I found his, which I'd sealed inside an envelope as if hiding it at the back of the attic wasn't sufficient concealment. Slitting the flap open, I remembered quite vividly in a sudden jolt of recall when I first put it in there. I was sitting in the kitchen of our old house in Manchester. Charlotte, who was nearly five, was in bed. It was only a few hours after my wife's funeral and I had seized gratefully on any activity that would take my mind off her death. The major task of packing up clothes and books had already been completed. Laura had died of cancer and, long before that, we both knew she had only months to live, so I'd had time in which to prepare for her death, including the arrangements to sell the house and buy this one in Northorpe. It was at her insistence that all these plans were made while she was still alive. To use her own words, she had wanted to be part of Charlotte's life, and mine, even after she was dead. So she had approved of the choice of school, Hillside, and had looked through the brochures from the estate agents.

'This one,' she had said with extraordinary positiveness, picking out Field Lodge, as if some intuitive knowledge was guiding her. She then had six more weeks to live but she sounded as excited as if she, too, was coming here to live with us, which in a way she was, for we both agreed that I would bring her ashes with us to Northorpe so that she could be buried near us. So far, I haven't carried out that last part of the agreement. I'm waiting until Charlotte is old enough to understand and then we'll bury her ashes together in the garden. In the meantime, her casket is locked away in the bottom drawer of the bureau in my bedroom, covered over with one of the silk scarves she loved wearing.

During her last illness, it was her courage and her fierce grip on the future that prevented me from breaking down. How could I, when she was so whole, so positive, so full of optimism about our future?

After she died, the only task that remained to be done on that final evening in

Manchester, apart from the last minute packing up before the arrival of the removal firm, was to empty my desk and sort through the remainder of the papers. The photographs were in a box in the bottom drawer. I remember spilling them out on to the kitchen table, choosing which ones to keep, which to discard.

I nearly threw away the photograph of M but at the last moment decided to keep it, so I put it instead into an envelope and sealed it up, thinking that he, too, was as good as buried. It was, I suppose, a token commitment of him, not to earth, but to oblivion.

Yet despite that, here I am now, slitting open the envelope and tipping the small oblong of slippery photographic paper on to the top of my desk.

It is a group photograph taken in the field behind the church in the Warwickshire village where my father was the vicar, after a summer fête to raise money for the repairs to the roof. In the background is the church itself, its square flint tower rising above the clumps of trees that marked the edge of the graveyard; chestnut trees, I remember, their leaves opening like green hands in the spring before the white flowers appeared, standing upright among the foliage like wax candles. Later in the autumn, I used to throw stones and pieces of dead wood into the branches to bring the conkers down when my father wasn't there to see me do it.

Against this background are standing the people who helped with the fête, M among them for he ran the Bowl-for-a-Pig competition, juggling the balls and shouting 'Roll up! Roll up!' like a proper fairground huckster. People liked him. He was jolly and made them laugh.

And there he is in the front row, of course—he would never take a back seat—and laughing. He is dressed casually in slacks and an open-necked shirt, and is leaning forward a little towards the camera, as if saying, 'Look at me! Here I am!' His fair hair is flopping in that schoolboy manner across his forehead and his head is tilted to one side in his usual breezy, self-confident way.

You can see immediately what he's like—cocksure, jaunty, and untrustworthy. Even I knew that although I was only ten at the time. And yet my mother fell in love with him and ran away with him to God knows here. My father never told me although perhaps he himself didn't know.

I never knew the circumstances that brought him to Kedstone, the village where my parents lived. But I can still vividly remember the day when I was told my mother had run away with him. It was a Saturday in April and my father had called me downstairs to breakfast, which was unusual. It was my mother who always woke me up. There was no sign of her when I went into the breakfast room, only my father standing at one end of the table, which was laid in a perfunctory manner with a packet of cornflakes, a jug of milk and my cereal bowl; no toast, no boiled egg, no glass dish of marmalade or my mother's homemade raspberry jam. And no sign of my mother.

My father simply said, 'Eat your breakfast, Peter, and then come and see me in my study. I want to talk to you.'

And with that he walked out of the room.

I ate some cornflakes but only a few, intimidated by the loud crunching noise I made in the empty room. My father's direction that I should have some breakfast, although said without any anger, was as good as a command. I remember feeling afraid; not so much of him but of the tension in the air, a great weight of dejection that told me something very grave had happened. It was nothing I had done. Had it been, he would have shown it in the way he fixed his eyes on me, like the time he caught me stealing currants from the jar in the kitchen.

It occurred to me that my mother's absence had something to do with it and I was very afraid that she was ill, dying perhaps, and I suddenly felt cold and hollow inside, as if my heart and stomach had dropped away into an empty pit.

My father was standing behind his desk when I knocked and was told to enter, his knuckles resting on its polished surface, his gaze directed towards me but not at me. Even now, all these years later, I can distinctly recall the look in his eyes. It was opaque, like that of a blind man, and his face had that strained, searching expression of someone who cannot see and, trapped in an unfamiliar room, is peering desperately about him for someone or some sign that might help him to find the way out.

It seemed a long time before he spoke, and when he did his voice sounded rusty, as if from disuse.

'I am sorry to have to tell you,' he said, his eyes still not meeting mine, 'that your mother has gone away.'

I did not understand.

'Gone away? Where to? When will she be coming back?'

A strange quiver passed over his face like a wind stirring the surface of a pond and he put one hand up to his mouth as if to control it. Then he looked down at the desk and said, 'She won't be coming back. Now go up to your room and pack some clothes for the weekend. You're going to stay at Mrs Grant's until Sunday evening.'

Nothing more was said. He simply turned his head towards the door to indicate I should leave, and I went out of the room.

I cannot really remember what I felt or thought. There is only that hollow feeling inside me when I recall that morning, a huge sense of loss and emptiness, and an overwhelming feeling of guilt, that, in some way I could not understand, it was my fault she had gone away.

I do remember walking about my bedroom, opening the wardrobe and the chest of drawers, wondering what to take with me to the Grants'. Pyjamas, I supposed, and clean socks. I could not think of anything else and finally I just sat on the edge of the bed, looking at the picture on the opposite wall of Jesus blessing the little children. The words 'Suffer little children to come unto me' were printed underneath it and I wondered again, as I always did, why Jesus should want the children to suffer. He looked so kind in the picture with His fair, softly curling hair and His hand held out towards them in an affectionate manner like a good, loving father. It crossed my mind that perhaps He was really asking them to pardon Him for making them suffer, although they looked happy, not sad, and that the outstretched hand was really meant as an appeal for forgiveness.

I was puzzling over this when there was a knock on the door and Mrs Grant came in. She was, and perhaps still is for all I know, a thin, bossy but kind-hearted woman, who played the organ at church and gave private piano lessons to local children, cycling to their houses on an old-fashioned bicycle, her thin, little legs in their lisle stockings pumping up and down on the pedals, her music case strapped to the carrier on the back.

She was obviously embarrassed at being put in charge of me and at a loss to know what to do so she covered up her awkwardness by bustling about finding additional things I hadn't thought to pack, such as slippers and a clean shirt and handkerchiefs. In the absence of anything to put them into, she folded them up into a parcel inside my dressing-gown, which she stuffed under her arm before taking me downstairs to the family car, which was parked outside the front door with Mr Grant, one of my father's churchwardens, at the wheel.

There was no sign of my father. As we drove away, I craned to look back at the house, expecting him to come out on to the steps to wave me goodbye, but he didn't appear. I didn't see him either over the weekend I stayed with the Grants.

Being childless, the Grants had no idea how to entertain a ten-year-old boy and on Saturday I was taken shopping with them to Tesco's, after I had been shown where I would sleep: a cramped room almost filled by a double bed and a vast wardrobe. In the afternoon, Mr Grant, a gingery, melancholy man who had obviously been told to entertain me, played draughts with me and then we watched television until bedtime. I remember lying rigid with misery in that huge bed, wondering where my mother was and when I would be going home.

On Sundays, I always attended Matins with my mother and, in the afternoons, I went alone to Sunday school, held in the Church Hall where Mrs Grant was one of the teachers. But that Sunday I remained closeted with Mr Grant who, instead of draughts, got out his boyhood stamp album to show me, turning the pages himself because I wasn't allowed to touch. Later, I helped him lay the table in the cold, north-facing dining room. I had the feeling they rarely used it, preferring to eat in the warm muddle of the kitchen but because I was the vicar's son and, moreover, the victim of a domestic tragedy, I had to be treated as a proper grown-up guest for Sunday dinner.

No one mentioned my mother, nor the reason for her sudden disappearance and it was not until the following week that I learned the truth from one of the children at school. Until that time, I had been protected by the teachers, a privilege I resented deeply because it marked me out as different from everyone else. At playtimes, I was kept in to help tidy the classroom bookshelves, pin up pupils' drawings on the walls or water the plants in the headmistress's room. Either my father or Mrs Grant escorted me to and from school at the beginning and end of the day, and in the dinner hour one of the women from the village, whose name I cannot now remember, came to the house to cook lunch for us and do other chores such as cleaning and washing.

It was only on the following Monday morning that this imposed purdah was lifted and I was allowed to join the other children in the playground. They were curious rather than unkind although some of them had that pleased I-know-something-you-don't-know look on their faces as they clustered round me in a little group.

'Is it true your mum's run off with that Mr M?' one of the girls asked, referring to him by his full name.

The realisation of what had really happened came as a shock but, once that initial feeling had passed, it was almost a relief to know the truth at last; for I knew it was the truth. I had seen them together, not often; they must have been very discreet. But there had been occasions when he'd call at the vicarage with some excuse or other when my father was not at home and they'd walked together in the garden. I had felt uneasy then for I was aware of a shared intimacy between them that I hadn't understood.

The girl's question also made it clear that other people in the village knew what had happened and had been discussing it among themselves. The thought that my mother was the subject of village gossip made me deeply ashamed. Both my parents were very scornful of gossip and always cut me short if I spoke of any tittle-tattle I'd heard at school.

When I got home that afternoon, I confronted my father with what I'd been told. I was afraid to do it but the need to hear him confirm or deny it was stronger than my fear.

He was silent for a long moment, his face averted, his profile closed and disapproving.

Then he said, still not looking at me, 'Yes, that is true, Peter'.

'But why?' I asked. 'Wasn't she happy here with us?'

Again there was a long silence before he replied and, when it came, the answer was deeply disturbing as well as unsatisfactory.

He said, 'Sometimes people think they'll be happier with someone else.'

And with that, he walked away.

So I still wasn't sure if my mother had really loved me or not. Or perhaps her love hadn't been strong enough. Or my love was not sufficient to make her want to stay with us.

There was also a troubling ambiguity in the way his answer was framed. 'Sometimes people *think* they'll be happier with someone else.' So they weren't sure either and that implied that love itself was uncertain.

My mother was never spoken of again. Her belongings, her clothes, her books, the pretty little things she'd placed about the house, disappeared, even the old coat hanging in the downstairs cloakroom, which she'd worn for gardening or to go blackberrying with me along the hedges. And as if to confirm the separation, my father moved out of the double bedroom at the front of the house into the spare room which contained only a single bed.

And then, two months later, when I was nearly eleven and should have been going to the grammar school in Warwick, I was sent away to a boys' boarding school for clergymen's sons in Suffolk and only came home for the long holidays. It was not only an exile but a punishment, I felt, for not being loved enough by my mother because I was unworthy of it.

There was one further twist to the story, which in part brought about a closure, to use the current word to describe an end to an emotional situation, although it was never really concluded. Two years later when I was home from school for the Easter holidays, there came a telephone call that my father took in his study. Soon afterwards he went upstairs, but I thought no more of the matter until, a little while later, I went upstairs myself to fetch a book I'd left on my bedside table.

The house was very quiet, a silence that was broken by a sound I'd never heard before, which came from behind the closed door of my father's room. It was a retching, coughing noise, such as a dog makes when it's trying to bring up something from its throat. I stood outside the door for several moments, listening to this disgusting sound that turned my stomach, wondering what to do. My father was ill, I thought, but I hesitated to go in to his room for fear of what I might find. And then I realised that he was crying and that what he was bringing up was not vomit but sobs, which he was spewing up from the very depths of his being.

I crept downstairs again and sat alone in the kitchen until my father came down and called me into his study. It was much the same as that other occasion when he told me my mother had left, only this time he was sitting at the desk, looking so haggard and worn that I was shocked by his appearance. He was suddenly an old man.

'I'm sorry to have to tell you,' he said, looking up at me but not seeing me at all, 'that your mother died last night.'

He said no more but got to his feet, which I took to be a signal to leave the room. But before I reached the door, he came round the desk towards me and suddenly, with no word or even an expression on his face to warn me what he was going to do, he put his arms around me and pulled me hard and close to his chest.

'I'm so sorry,' he repeated. I could feel his breath on the top of my head. Then he added, 'We won't speak of it again.'

Then he released me and walked over to the window where he stood, looking out, his back towards me.

He was as good as his word and we never mentioned my mother again although, for my father, the closure was not completed until the following day, when Mrs Grant and a friend of hers, Miss Armitage, who helped clean the church brasses, came to the house and emptied the wardrobe and the chest of drawers in the double bedroom of her clothes, which were packed into carrier bags and driven away in Miss Armitage's Morris Minor. Everything was taken, even the jars and bottles on the dressing-table. I believe they went to a charity shop in Warwick.

Later that same night my father performed his own ritual closure. It was about half past eleven. I was in bed and should have been asleep when I heard my father walk through the house to the kitchen and then the sound of the back door opening and closing. My bedroom overlooked the back garden and, scrambling quickly out of bed, I went to the window without turning on the light. Opening the curtains a little, I peered out and saw my father carrying a cardboard box in his hands, walking down the lawn to the far end of the garden where there was a vegetable plot.

It was too dark to see exactly what he was doing but I could just make out his form as he bent down and put the box on the ground. Seconds later, a little light sprang up as a match was struck and the tiny flame was carried with great care downwards, where it hovered for a moment like a moth before growing in strength and brightness. Almost at once, the box and its contents caught fire and the flames spurted upwards. In their shifting light, I saw my father take a step backwards and then remain standing motionless, looking down at the flames. When they died down, he turned and came walking back to the house.

By the time he had entered the house and closed the kitchen door, I was back in bed, listening in the darkness as both bolts were shot home and the lights were turned off downstairs. A narrow slit of brightness suddenly appeared under my bedroom door as the landing light was switched on, and then that, too, vanished as he went into his bedroom and closed the door behind him.

It was a long time before I went to sleep. I lay there wondering what it was he had burnt so surreptitiously in the garden, and the following morning, a Sunday, after he'd left the house to take eight o'clock Communion, I went down to the vegetable garden to look.

Very little remained of the bonfire. It was mostly grey ash and darker flakes of charred paper, amongst which whole unburnt fragments remained, large enough for me to make out what they were. They were parts of letters from my mother. I recognised the handwriting. On some of them whole words had survived the fire.

The rest were burnt scraps of photographs on which nothing was recognisable. It was only the glossy surface on some of them that distinguished them from the rest.

There was, however, a postscript to that episode. After my father's death, I found an envelope in the locked bottom drawer of his desk containing those photographs I brought with me to Northorpe and hid in the attic of the house. Presumably these remaining photographs were too precious or too significant for him to destroy along with all the others, although I wondered why he had kept the group photo that included M. Was it a form of masochism to remind himself of his wife's betrayal? Or to punish himself for some shortcoming on his part that had driven her away?

God knows. I sometimes wonder if he understood it himself.

The ritual burning prompted me to perform a ritual of my own devising although in this case it was more of an occult rite and I had no difficulty in recognising the motive behind it.

It was several days before I carried out the ceremony. First I had to collect up all the objects I would need. I also had to be sure my father would be out of the house. In the event, I had to wait nearly a week before he left to drive into Warwick to visit an elderly parishioner in hospital there. I knew it would be over an hour before he came home.

He was uneasy about leaving me alone in the house but I protested I was old enough—nearly thirteen—so he gave in, only reluctantly as if he guessed I had some secret plan to carry out while he was away. So I waited for quarter of an hour after he drove off just in case he came back and found I had gone.

When the time was up, I hurriedly collected the box containing all the components I would need for my own ritual, which I had hidden in the back of my wardrobe. It was an oblong tin, which had once contained shortbread and which had a picture of a Scotty dog on the lid wearing a tartan Glengarry cap; extraordinary that after all these years I can still recall that image so clearly. Stuffing it into the saddle-bag on my bike, I rode off.

I knew exactly where I was going. About half a mile down the road, there was—and possibly still is, unless it's been cut down to make way for a housing estate—a wood known as Hangman's Grove where, or so it was said, a man had hanged himself after he had accidentally shot dead his brother when they were out rabbiting together. Even the tree had been identified—a large oak that stood by itself in a little glade where, in spring, the grass was thick with primroses and bluebells. It's a place of beauty rather than ugliness but its legend of violent death drew me to it.

I half rode, half carried the bike through the undergrowth until the bushes grew too dense, when I finally abandoned it behind a clump of bracken. After that, I went the rest of the way on foot, the tin under my arm.

I have no memory of consciously learning about black magic. I must have picked up the knowledge little by little from books and comics and schoolboy gossip. But I knew roughly what the ritual should consist of.

Once I'd arrived at the oak tree, I chose a place where two great roots came thrusting out of the ground like giant hands, forming a bowl-shaped hollow between them in the ground. Unpacking the box, I carefully laid out the objects I had brought with me inside this hollow, as if on an altar. First the penknife, then the candle ends, the piece of slate, the box of matches, some newspaper, some pins fastened to a scrap of cloth, an old trowel, the lid of a cocoa tin that I'd taken from the dustbin and scrubbed clean and, lastly, a smooth stone that I'd found in the garden, which I'd also scrubbed clean and which was the size and shape of a duck's egg. That done, I collected up dry twigs and leaves for the fire, which I placed in a little pile between the roots on top of a sheet of the newspaper, crumpled up into a ball. I then cut up the candle ends into smaller pieces, put them into the tin lid, which in turn I placed on the trowel. Holding the matchbox carefully as if it was something precious, I struck a match and carried the flame down to my little bonfire, conscious that

I was repeating the same actions my father had performed in the garden a few days before.

The flame guttered a little and I was afraid it would go out. If it did, the magic would not work. But, as I cradled it in my cupped hand, it steadied and grew stronger and, when I touched it to the paper, it flared into life, running like a stream of yellow and blue fire through the twigs and dry leaves and sending up a thin plume of white smoke.

Very, very carefully I picked up the trowel, which held the lid of broken candle pieces, and lowered it over the flames, watching the scraps of candle begin to lose their shape and form soft, malleable lumps in a pool of molten wax.

I was worried that I had nothing of M's to add to the wax, ideally some of his hair or better still some nail clippings. But in their absence, I did the best I could and chanted M's name as the scraps of candle swam together and finally dissolved.

Once they had become liquid, I lifted the trowel from the fire and let it cool a little until a skin formed. Then, taking the penknife, I scraped the softened wax onto the slate, which served as my modelling board.

I was surprised how quickly the wax began to cool and harden, although it remained hot enough to burn the tips of my fingers as I scooped it up and began to mould it between my hands like plasticine, still chanting 'M!M!M!' under my breath.

70

The finished mannikin was crude, little more than sausage-shaped rolls, a big one for the body, four smaller ones for the arms and legs, a round ball for the head. There was not enough wax to make the legs long enough and they looked like little stumps, cut off at the knees. But the head was good. It even had a small nose and chin which I'd pinched out between my fingers when the wax was still malleable. A few quick jabs with the blade of my penknife formed the mouth and eyes.

And then came the climax of the ritual. I picked up the three pins I'd laid out on the tree root and drove them home, one into the head of the little wax figure, one into the stomach and the last one into the place where the heart would be. I then sat back on my heels to examine my handiwork. It was incomplete, I felt, looking at it critically. Something was missing, which the hair or nail parings would have supplied. Or, even better, blood.

It was then this idea came to me to turn the ritual into a sacrifice. Cleaning the blade of the penknife with a handful of grass, I drew the tip of it across the end of my little finger, just deep enough to break the skin. Blood oozed out in big, round, red drops, which I gathered up on the end of the matchstick and, using it like a pencil, I drew the initial M on the mannikin's chest.

It was finished and I was deeply satisfied. All that remained was to bury my sacrifice, which I did under the site of the fire, laying the little wax figure in the hole I had dug out with the trowel before filling it in with a mixture of earth, ash and the charcoal remains of the twigs. On top of it, I laid the stone.

I stood over the grave for several long minutes, thinking of M and my dead mother, who was also buried somewhere in the ground, only I didn't know where.

Even now, I find it difficult to describe my feelings. They were a mixture of exultation and grief and loss. But mostly they were of rage and hate for M, which, like a clean bright flame, seemed to burn away all other emotions. I certainly felt no guilt.

Before I left, I cleared up all the evidence of what I had done, putting the objects I'd brought with me into the biscuit tin. On the way home, I dropped it into a rubbish bin by the bus stop on the outskirts of the village.

As far as I know, the grave is still there under the oak tree in Hangman's Grove. The last time I looked for it was ten years ago, after my father died and was buried in the graveyard of St Saviour's church at his special wish, even though it was almost twenty years since he'd served as its parish priest.

After the funeral, I drove to Hangman's Grove and found the place where I had buried the wax image of M. The stone was still there, nestling among the young grass and bright yellow celandines, their petals as shiny as wax themselves.

I had no desire to disinter the little mannikin. But I remember thinking that I couldn't make the same ritual visit to my mother's grave. As he lay dying, my father told me that she had committed suicide after M had abandoned her for another woman. He hadn't told me where she was buried. Perhaps he didn't know; and I didn't like to ask.

It was a closure of a sort.

Of M, I know nothing. He, too, may be dead. If he is, then that should have been the end of it and I should have laid it all aside. And I would have done, if Murray hadn't come into my life.

Wednesday, 2nd July.

I haven't seen Murray since I lent him the material on Northorpe Hall. Or Jocelyn, come to that, although late yesterday afternoon I saw her car parked in front of Murray's house when I was driving past on my way back from Thurston after a meeting with the surveyor and the builder about the barn conversion. The plan is to start next week, stripping off the tiles and any roof timbers that need replacing.

I hadn't intended to spy on Murray but I couldn't resist the temptation of slowing down when I was nearing his place. The drive gates were open and there was her Renault parked outside the front door. It had to be hers. No one else I know of owns a car in that particular shade of metallic red.

It's none of my business and in some ways I'm relieved that Murray has taken her off my hands. But if she's hoping for a steady, lasting relationship with Murray, then she's looking in the wrong place. He'll dump her sooner or later, as M dumped my mother.

Knowing Jocelyn, I doubt if she'd kill herself if Murray did dump her. She's tougher than that. But she'd be hurt, that's for certain.

Oddly enough, Jocelyn phoned me this morning out of the blue. I've noticed before that if you think of someone, quite soon afterwards he or she turns up. I don't think there's anything supernatural or extrasensory about it; it's just coincidence, but when it happens you are startled by it.

She was phoning, she said, to find out how I was. It was ages since she'd seen me. Could we meet up for a drink and a chat?

Her voice sounded higher-pitched than usual and tense.

'What about next Thursday evening?' I suggested.

'Oh, that's ages away!' she protested. 'Are you free this evening?'

So whatever it was she wanted to chat about, it was urgent and also apparently confidential, for when I suggested the Feathers in the village, she said, 'Not there. People might overhear us. What about the Wheatsheaf in Bullingham?'

'All right,' I agreed. 'Shall we say eight o'clock?'

In some ways, it was a damn nuisance. I wanted to push on with the plans for the barn but I was also curious to find out what she wanted to talk to me about. I guessed it was Murray and I decided not to get too involved. I would simply listen to what she had to say. At the same time, mean-spirited though it is, I wanted to know more about him, especially negative information to confirm my dislike of the man.

Jocelyn had toned herself down for the occasion—no jewellery, only a little make-up and a loose-fitting blouse over her jeans so as not to show off her figure and be too conspicuous. And she insisted we took our drinks out into the garden where we sat at one of the rustic tables well away from the windows of the pub. It was a cool evening and, apart from us, the garden was empty, so we drew attention to ourselves by being the only couple out there. And despite her obvious attempt to look inconspicuous, her behaviour was hardly low key. She leaned conspiratorially across the table, one hand close to her mouth even though no one could have overheard us.

She began with a few bright conversational questions. How was I? How was my work going? And inevitably, How was Charlotte?

I answered briefly—I was fine; so was Charlotte; the work was going along

75

splendidly—while I waited for her to get to the real purpose of our meeting.

It came eventually and, as I had suspected, it was about Murray.

Had I seen him recently? she asked.

'No, I haven't,' I replied, which was true, in a way. It was over a week since I'd called on him with the information on Northorpe Hall and I had no intention of telling her about that meeting with him, a decision I couldn't properly explain even to myself. But I felt instinctively that it would be unwise to link myself too closely with Murray.

Her next question astounded me.

'Has he ever mentioned Mrs Gunter?'

'No, he hasn't. Why do you ask? Is something the matter?'

She looked disappointed, as if I had let her down by not giving her the right answer. But she couldn't let it go.

'Nothing really,' she replied in an off-hand voice. 'It's just that he's been seeing her recently. I've seen his car a couple of times outside her house.'

I should have left it there but I couldn't help adding, 'Surely you don't think they're having an affair? She must be in her seventies.'

The colour rushed into her face and I felt ashamed and angry with myself for goading her. To make amends, I added, taking care not to mention my uneasiness at seeing him paying court to Mrs Gunter at Jocelyn's party, 'I imagine it's business, Jocelyn. He's a financial adviser, isn't he? He's probably advising her on her stocks and shares or whatever.'

'You think so?' She sounded relieved.

'I'm certain of it,' I assured her.

After that, thank God, the conversation moved from Murray to other topics, mostly to do with her and her life: her boutique, a problem with a supplier, village gossip. But Murray was evidently still on her mind because as we said goodbye in the car-park, she added, just before she started the engine and drove off, 'You know, he's enormous fun to be with'.

As a parting shot, it was curious. She was obviously speaking of Murray, but why refer to him in that way? Was it to rouse my jealousy? Or to remind herself of his charm? Or to excuse his interest in Mrs Gunter, or hers in him? I wasn't sure and I had the feeling Jocelyn didn't know either.

Thursday, 3rd July.

Tomorrow Charlotte will be here and I've planned something very special for her. I thought I'd take her to Westbrook House on Saturday. It's a large Victorian mansion that has only been open to the public for a few weeks. It belonged to a very old lady who died about two years ago, leaving the house to the National Trust. It's still exactly as it was when she was a child—carpets, furniture, everything, even down to the kitchen equipment and the maids' rooms. I've been told it's a time capsule and stepping over the threshold is like walking back into the 1900s. I'm sure Charlotte will love it, especially the exhibition of Victorian toys in the nursery. The gardens are also worth seeing, I've heard. They've been restored and there's a formal rose garden that I'd like Charlotte to see with me as it may give us some ideas for our own rose garden.

It's about twenty miles away and I thought we'd have lunch at the Swan in Sandham—it's a lovely old pub—and tea at Westbrook House after we've looked round the place. The original coach house has been turned into a restaurant.

Sunday, 6th July. Evening.

I've just arrived home having picked Fiona up from the Bradshaws' and driven her and Charlotte back to Hillside. I was sorry Derek Bradshaw, Fiona's father, wasn't there. I wanted to thank him for bringing Charlotte home on Friday afternoon. Evidently he was calling on a client in the area so he offered to give her a lift here instead of her having to wait for the bus, which was kind of him. It's a pity he's so antisocial. I would have liked to ask him in for a drink but he was obviously in a hurry to get away.

Something very disturbing happened this afternoon. We had taken Charlotte's plans for the rose garden outside to the patio, where we were sitting discussing them when the gate opened and Murray walked in, carrying the Northorpe Hall folder. I wasn't expecting him; he hadn't phoned to ask if he could call. Had he done so, I would have said no. I don't like other people being around when Charlotte is at home. I'm not sure why. It's utterly irrational but I feel I must keep her safe and not let in any intruders.

He came towards us smiling and something about his smile and the way he held his head convinced me that he'd come deliberately without any warning in order to meet Charlotte. I've made a point of never mentioning to him that I have a daughter so I knew who must have told him. Jocelyn, of course. She had probably described her as very young and pretty. And, knowing Jocelyn, she almost certainly added in that sweet, sentimental voice of hers that I hate, 'She's profoundly deaf. Isn't it a shame?'

So he had prepared his expression and also, I suspected, his opening remarks as well.

'Oh, I'm so sorry, Alex,' he said, using my Christian name for the first time, another deliberate ploy to create the impression, for Charlotte's benefit presumably, that he and I are more intimate than is the case. 'If I'd known you were busy, I wouldn't have come.'

Clever that, also, suggesting he was sensitive enough not to wish to intrude.

I introduced them very briefly.

79

'Charlotte, this is Noel Murray. Noel, my daughter Charlotte.'

I was angry that I was forced to use his Christian name myself, reinforcing the impression of intimacy between us.

I spoke his name rather than signing it for her so as not to emphasise her deafness, which I deliberately wanted to play down. I didn't want his pity any more than Jocelyn's.

He smiled and nodded at her, his face expressing nothing more than a kindly interest in her and pleasure at their meeting. He was also clever enough to contrive an invitation from me to sit down.

Moving closer to the table, he laid the folder down in front of one of the empty chairs, remarking as he did so, 'Thank you so much, Alex, for lending me all this material. It's absolutely fascinating.' Indicating the chair, he added, 'May I?'

Hardly waiting for my nod of acceptance— after all, what else could I do?—he addressed Charlotte directly, speaking slowly and clearly.

'Do you know the ruins of Northorpe Hall? Has Alex taken you to see them?'

So he knew, probably again through Jocelyn, that Charlotte can lip read. But what he clearly wasn't prepared for was the manner in which Charlotte reads other people's lips. She has to watch each movement very closely, her attention fixed solely on the person addressing her. To someone not used to it, that close scrutiny can be disturbing, especially as Charlotte's eyes are intensely blue, the irises patterned with small flecks of gold and darker blue like opals. Some people are made self-conscious by that bright, direct gaze; others are flattered by it, assuming Charlotte is fascinated by them.

Murray, of course, belonged to the latter group. Assured of his own good looks, he immediately concluded that Charlotte found him attractive. But what I wasn't prepared for and which shocked me profoundly was the sudden jolt of sexual excitement that she aroused in him. It was as if an electric charge had jumped across the space between them and was almost palpable. The air seemed to grow more dense, as if it had been compressed, and I felt this pressure on my eardrums as happens on a plane when it gains height and the hearing becomes muffled, distancing one from one's surroundings. My breathing became difficult and when I tried to speak, it was an enormous physical effort to force my throat and mouth to form the sounds.

I said, and the words seemed to come from a great distance, 'No, I haven't taken Charlotte to the ruins. The place is so overgrown, it's quite dangerous.'

The triteness of the remark seemed to break the enchantment, as I'd hoped it would. Charlotte, who had turned her attention from Murray to me, smiled and shook her head at me in a teasing manner. It was a moment of intimacy between just the two of us—a reminder of my over-protective behaviour towards her, and she made one of our private gestures which you wouldn't find in a manual of sign language for the deaf. It's a rapid flapping movement of her elbows and means, 'Stop fussing over me like a mother hen'.

Murray, eager to include himself in our magic circle, was saying, 'I must have a look at it myself as soon as I can. Is it private property?'

'Yes, it is,' I replied. 'It's owned jointly by several heirs but two of them live abroad and apparently none of them can agree on what to do with it.'

'I'm surprised they haven't sold it long ago for redevelopment. The site must be worth small fortune.'

His remarks struck a sour note in the conversation and I saw Charlotte, who was again watching his lips attentively, shrink a little into herself at this overtly pecuniary response and he was quick to withdraw.

'But of course,' Murray continued, speaking slowly for her benefit, 'the ruins are too beautiful to be pulled down. They ought to be preserved before they deteriorate any further.'

Charlotte smiled and nodded agreement and Murray had the sense to leave while he was in her good books.

Getting to his feet, he held out his hand first

to me and then to her. His hand was warm and firm. When he took Charlotte's, I looked closely at her while her attention was on him, wondering what sort of effect he had on her.

He was certainly good-looking. The shadow cast by the sun umbrella over the table made his features appear more dramatic than in full sunlight, highlighting the bone structure. I had to admit that there was a certain distinguished air about him, his lean, dark features suggesting someone of an intellectual nature, interested in books and ideas, someone trustworthy and mature.

Charlotte's face gave nothing away. She has that capacity which many deaf people possess of assuming a smiling but non-committal expression on occasions, as if her deafness has given her a privacy and isolation that covers her like a veil.

After Murray had left, a silence fell which I should have accepted as an end to the encounter. But perversely I couldn't let it go.

I signed to her, 'What did you think of him?'

She looked at me a little surprised that I should want to know. Then she made a gesture which I've never seen her make before. It was entirely spontaneous.

Using her right hand, she drew a circle round her face and then, with her left, she touched her chin and made a lifting movement, as if she were peeling an invisible face away. At the same time, she raised her eyebrows and shoulders, frowning interrogatively as she did so.

The pantomime was quite clear. She was questioning whether the persona Murray presented to the world was genuine or false, and if false, then what was the man's true personality?

I should have been comforted by this mime of hers but at the same time I was disturbed by it for, while it suggested she was uncertain whether he was trustworthy or not, she was also interested enough in him to be intrigued by what she saw. Indifference would have been more comforting.

Sunday 20th July.

I have seen nothing of Murray for over two weeks but feel that isn't the last of the man. As a result, I've been very tense, expecting him to drop by casually this weekend as he did the last time Charlotte was at home. So, in order to avoid another meeting, I took her to Suffolk, booking rooms for us at a hotel in Aldeburgh and driving down there on Friday soon after she arrived home.

We went to the usual tourist places, including a visit to the Moot Hall which now, because of coastal erosion, is stranded on the beach, like a Tudor boat that has been pulled on to the shore and left there when the tide went out.

Afterwards, we walked along the coast to

Dunwich and then on to Walberswick, where we had lunch at the Bell.

Both of us love this area of Suffolk—the sea and the huge skies and the flat stretches of glistening marshes. It has a clarity of light that is like crystal and the air is clean and cold like dry white wine. At times such as that, I regret Charlotte's deafness deeply. I wish passionately she could hear the surge and roar of the waves and the wind seething in the reed beds and the screams of the sea gulls as they are caught and tossed upwards by the air currents; even small noises like the chinking sound of the stays in the rigging of the boats at anchor in the estuary.

She looked so beautiful on that walk along the coast, her hair wild, her skin and eyes brilliant from the freshness of the air.

She caught me looking at her and smiled, tilting her head enquiringly.

I said, 'I love you.'

Reading my lips, she laughed and silently replied, 'I love you too'.

Taking my arm, she hugged it close to her side.

And so we walked together, the two of us, and I thought I hadn't been so happy for a long, long time.

Part Two

CHAPTER ONE

'Northorpe,' Finch announced, reading aloud from the sign placed low on the verge on the left-hand side of the road.

He hadn't intended the remark to be significant, but Detective Sergeant Helen Wyatt, the replacement for Tom Boyce, the DS, now retired, who in the past had usually accompanied the Detective Chief Inspector on his investigations, promptly slowed down to under 30 miles an hour but made no comment herself, which pleased him.

She was an attractive young woman in her early thirties: unmarried, as Finch had discovered from her file, although he believed there was a partner somewhere around. If there was, she never spoke of him. Or perhaps her. These days you couldn't be sure.

Some of her colleagues found her a little too self-contained for their taste but he liked her air of separateness and cool efficiency, an impression which was borne out by her physical appearance: dark hair cut short as if tailored to fit her head; trim figure; well-modelled features. Whenever he caught an unexpected glimpse of her profile, it reminded him of a face on a Roman coin. It had the same purity of outline.

And, best of all, she was sensitive to his

moods, unlike Boyce who, under similar circumstances, would have felt the need to respond to Finch's remark, disturbing his train of thought. Helen kept silent, thank God.

At the beginning of any enquiry, especially this one, which involved the disappearance of a fourteen-year-old school girl who was, moreover, profoundly deaf, he needed to have his mind quite clear, like an unused film in a camera on which he could imprint those vital first impressions before all the other data connected with the case came crowding in on him.

First the setting.

He had heard of Northorpe. In fact, he'd driven through it on several occasions while engaged on other investigations and had consequently not paid particular attention to it. He made good that omission now, setting the shutter of his mind wide open, so to speak, and concentrating on his surroundings which, with Helen Wyatt at the wheel, he could do without any distractions.

His first impression was one of middle-class affluence. Everything, including the grass verges, was neat and well-maintained, as if someone that very morning had gone round with mop and hoover, cleaning and polishing and tidying up. There was not a scrap of litter lying about. Windows gleamed. Even the pavements looked scrubbed. And there were flowers everywhere—in window-boxes and hanging-baskets on most of the houses while the Feathers, the local pub, beamed and plastered, looked like a vertical herbaceous border, dripping with geraniums and petunias and that fancy, silver-leaved plant, much loved by municipal gardeners, the name of which he didn't know.

No council houses, he noticed. Like the litter, they had probably been tidied away, out of sight of the village centre, into a side-turning. But it gave him perverse pleasure to note two eyesores—a couple of squat, pebble-dashed bungalows and a pair of tiny clapboard cottages huddled together shoulder to shoulder at the side of the road without any benefit of gardens, let alone floral displays.

Northorpe also seemed to cater more than adequately for its residents' spiritual as well as physical needs. There was a flint church, St Peter's, with an imposing tower; a red-brick and slate chapel; and a general grocer's cum post-office plus off-licence. Like the pub, the shop was lavishly decorated with the ubiquitous window-boxes and tubs of flowers.

That middle-class affluence was particularly apparent in the houses themselves, many of which were Victorian or Edwardian detached villas, shielded from the common gaze by trees and shrubbery.

Alex Lambert's house, which was on the far side of the village on the Foxton road, was similarly hidden, but Finch had the impression that the barrier of leaves and branches were part of the original hedge, which had not been torn out when the house was built. It was a natural planting of hawthorn and briar, trimmed back it was true, but not prettified by the addition of suburban lilacs and laburnums.

An ordinary five-barred gate, such as one would find on a farm, with the name-plate, Field Lodge, fastened to the top rail, was closed and Finch had to get out to open it before they could set off up the drive. As he waited at the gate opening for Helen Wyatt to turn right into the entrance, he glanced up and down the road and caught a glimpse of the top of a white-painted gable-end further down on the left, just visible above the trees and hedges that bordered both sides of the road.

As far as he could make out, it was the only house in sight.

Field Lodge had the same unspoilt, rural feel about it as the hedge that fronted it. A square box of a place, built of pinkish-red bricks rubbed with age, it had a slate roof that came down low over the upper storey, giving it a withdrawn, secretive air, an impression magnified by a very old, gnarled wisteria that clambered over the façade, its tendrils reaching up to the gutter, and by the fact that the blinds over the downstairs windows were lowered.

Finch assumed that it had once been a game-keeper's cottage or a farm bailiff's. It was too large for a labourer's.

He was also struck by the solitude and silence of the place. Apart from that one house further down the road, there were no near neighbours. It could have been miles from anywhere, and it crossed Finch's mind that Alex Lambert might have chosen it for this very reason.

So far he knew very little about the man, only a few basic facts passed on by Bridger, the local sergeant, who had interviewed Lambert when he had first reported his daughter missing. He was, Finch gathered, an architect who worked from home; also a widower, the missing girl his only child. She was fourteen and deaf. The fact that she was handicapped and was a minor had rung alarm bells at Divisional Headquarters at Chelmsford and an investigation had been set in motion straight away. Search parties, backed up by a helicopter, were already combing the route she had taken when she went missing and plain-clothes officers were calling at any houses along the way for potential witnesses who might have seen or heard something.

According to a statement taken from Alex Lambert by DS Bridger, the girl apparently caught a bus from the village of Foxton about five miles away where she had been visiting a schoolfriend, a fellow pupil at Hillside, a boarding school for the deaf at Banfield, and should have got off at the bus stop on the outskirts of Northorpe which was, in fact, a mere thirty yards down the road from her house. However, the bus had broken down at Hoe Green, a village about a mile and a quarter along the road from Northorpe, where the driver had phoned the depot to report the incident. A replacement bus had been sent out but, rather than wait for it to arrive, the girl had decided to walk the rest of the way home. She never arrived. Somewhere along that mile and a quarter stretch of road between Hoe Green and Field Lodge she had disappeared.

Alex Lambert, who had expected her off the bus at 4.55, had waited for a quarter of an hour and then had telephoned the Bradshaws' house where his daughter Charlotte had been visiting Fiona Bradshaw. Mrs Bradshaw had collected both girls from the school at the end of afternoon lessons and had taken them back to her house in Foxton to have tea together, a routine arrangement that took place every other Friday afternoon. Mrs Bradshaw had told Alex Lambert that Charlotte had caught the Northorpe bus at 4.25 as intended; in fact, she had seen her get on it. The bus stop was almost outside the Bradshaws' house. She had then heard the bus drive off.

At that stage, no one knew about the breakdown at Hoe Green.

Alex Lambert, alarmed by his daughter's non-arrival, had got in his car and driven along the Foxton road and had come across the stranded bus, together with its driver and passengers, waiting at the side of the road at Hoe Green. It was from the driver and some of the passengers that Alex Lambert learned that a young girl, answering Charlotte's description, had walked off down the road in the direction of Northorpe. According to a couple of them, they had tried to persuade the girl to wait for the replacement but she apparently hadn't understood what they were saying, no doubt because of her deafness, which they weren't aware of at the time.

Lambert had immediately driven home and telephoned the police to report her missing which might, under normal circumstances, have been considered an over-reaction. But from the outset, the situation was regarded as serious. Quite apart from her deafness and the fact that she was a minor, she had no money on her apart from a small amount of change. Moreover, there was no reason for her to run away from home. The circumstances of her disappearance were disturbing and, from the beginning, the possibility of abduction was taken seriously.

It was an aspect of the case that Finch and Helen Wyatt had discussed on their way to Northorpe. Neither of them had yet raised the possibility of murder, although it was on both their minds.

Seeing the house where Charlotte Lambert lived had given Finch further disquiet. It

95

reminded him of the fairy-tale he had read as a child about a beautiful young girl—Rapunzel, wasn't it?—who had been shut away in a tower to hide her from the many suitors who wished to marry her. And Charlotte Lambert was certainly beautiful. He had seen a photograph of her. DS Bridger had asked for one when he first interviewed Alex Lambert so that, if necessary, leaflets and posters could be printed reporting her missing without delay.

Finch had a copy of it in his pocket and, as he glanced at it again and was reminded of her features—the smooth forehead, the calm oval of her face, the wide-set eyes—he wondered if the same motive, unconscious perhaps, had lain behind Lambert's choice of this particular house. Was it to hide her from the outside world?

It was time to meet the man.

There was no bell on the front door, only an iron ring shaped like a coil of rope, probably original and too heavy to use discreetly. As Finch knocked on the door with it, the noise was disconcertingly loud. Birds started up in the surrounding shrubbery and one, a blackbird, fled into the bushes, scolding loudly.

'Oh, hell!' Finch muttered under his breath and then re-arranged his expression as footsteps were heard approaching. A man's voice called out aggressively from behind the closed door.

'Who is it?'

'The police,' Finch called back, exchanging a quizzical glance with Helen, who raised her shoulders in reply.

'Just a minute,' the man replied in a less belligerent tone.

There followed a rattle of bolts being drawn and a chain being removed before the door opened.

Alex Lambert was not quite what Finch had expected. He had imagined someone tall, lean and dark, perhaps a little dour but professional-looking, like a lawyer or a bank manager. What he saw was a man in his forties, of medium height, with light brown hair, turning grey, cut close to his head, and a small, trimmed beard of the same colour and texture. The features, while pleasant enough, were drawn and tense—with grief at his daughter's disappearance, Finch assumed, although he had the impression that Lambert would always hold himself aloof from other people, never exposing his true nature to outsiders.

Without speaking, Lambert held the door open and gestured to them to enter with a curt movement of his head before closing and locking the door behind them. In the shuffling about in the hall that followed, Finch and Helen standing aside to let Lambert lead the way, the Chief Inspector had a moment to look about him.

At the end of the passage was a door, its

upper half glazed with squares of coloured glass through which the sunlight cast a blue and yellow chequer-board pattern on the red quarry-tiled floor.

To his left, through an open door, he also caught a brief glimpse of a room in which the blinds were lowered and was in semi-darkness, although he could just make out some office equipment, mostly a large draughtsman's drawing board, tilted at an angle, its table taking up most of the space. Other pieces of apparatus stood on shelves and the tops of cupboards, including a word processor and its printer. There was no time to observe any more details. Lambert, who had gone ahead, was holding open another door on the right at the end of the passage.

It led into a large room, the front part of which appeared to be furnished as a dining room, the rear half, through which they had entered, as a sitting room. The blinds in both rooms were also drawn and the sunlight filtering through the beige-coloured linen filled them with a subdued, creamy glow, which made it difficult to make out details. With a muttered apology, Lambert went over to the window in the back half and released the blind, which shot up with a rattle, revealing the interior of both rooms.

They were startling in their simplicity— plain white walls, pine floorboards polished to a high gloss, a minimum of furniture. They were too austere for Finch's taste but he assumed they reflected Lambert's personality: no frills, no fuss, just the barest necessities; a monkish attitude which no doubt explained his lack of explanation for the lowered blinds, although Finch thought he could guess the reason. Not only did they prevent anyone from looking in, they also isolated Lambert from the outside world; further evidence, he felt, for what he was beginning to think of as the Rapunzel Syndrome.

'Please sit down,' Lambert was saying.

He himself remained standing by the fireplace, empty except for a huge stoneware jug filled with wild flowers and grasses, the only decoration in the entire room apart from a rug of rough apricot-coloured wool that lay in front of the hearth.

Finch opened the interview. He felt it was important to establish his authority from the outset. Having now met Lambert, he guessed instinctively that he would take charge, given the opportunity. There was an air of control about the man and he wondered how far this attitude extended to his relationship with his daughter.

'I'm sorry we couldn't give you prior notice of our visit,' he said, as he and Helen seated themselves on one of two sofas, covered in black and white ticking, which were drawn up at right angles to the fireplace. 'I did try to telephone but the phone appears to be disconnected.'

'Yes, it is. I didn't want to be bothered with people ringing up to commiserate.' Lambert sounded bitter, as if angered by such demonstrations of sympathy. Then he added abruptly, 'Is there any news?'

'I'm sorry; I'm afraid there isn't,' Finch replied. 'They're searching along the road from Hoe Green but nothing's been found yet.'

Nothing's been found yet, Finch thought. How we use language to disguise the truth! He wished he had the courage to answer Lambert's question honestly by saying: 'No, we haven't found your daughter's body,' which was what the man wanted to know.

Lambert nodded as if accepting Finch's reply but he still needed to have the truth put into words.

Looking the Chief Inspector straight in the face, he asked, his voice harsh, 'I suppose there's very little chance that she's still alive?'

Finch felt Helen shift uncomfortably beside him on the sofa and he himself had to summon up the control not to let his feelings show either in his face or in his voice.

'It's possible.'

Lambert still wouldn't let it go.

'But unlikely?' he persisted.

'It's early days, Mr Lambert. We haven't yet established what happened after she left the bus at Hoe Green.'

'She was abducted,' Lambert said, with conviction.

It was Finch's own conclusion, but he felt obliged to act as devil's advocate.

'We don't know that yet.'

'It's the only possible explanation. She hasn't run away. She had no reason to. She's happy here with me and at school. And apart from that, she's profoundly deaf, for God's sake! Besides, she had hardly any money on her. And where the hell would she go?'

Finch could hear barely controlled rage and despair in Lambert's voice, overlaid with an unexpected tone of self-contempt, as if the man was repelled by his own emotion.

There was a silence until Finch, anxious to move the interview away from this difficult area, went on, 'If a stranger offered Charlotte a lift in a car, would she have accepted it?'

'From a stranger? No!' Lambert sounded quite positive.

'What if it was someone she knew?'

The question seemed to strike the man in an unexpected manner. Instead of replying immediately, he held Finch's gaze for a couple of moments and then looked away.

'She might, I suppose,' he replied, but not sounding very convinced.

It was a strange reaction, neither a positive yes or no. Lambert could, of course, be unsure himself how his daughter might behave in such circumstances, never having had to consider it before. Curious over the man's hesitation, Finch decided to follow the subject up.

'How many people does she know in the village?'

'Well, I suppose she knows quite a few by sight. She's been a boarder at Hillside School for the Deaf at Banfield for the past nine years but she comes home every other weekend. If I go into the village to the shop or the post office, she always comes with me. I've also taken her to the Feathers a number of times for lunch and we frequently drive through the village on our way to Chelmsford for example.'

'These would be mainly acquaintances,' Finch pointed out. 'What about people she might have closer contact with, such as your own friends?'

'I'm not particularly close to anyone,' Lambert replied. He sounded on the defensive. 'I know a few people fairly well. We meet from time to time for drinks or a dinner party, but I don't encourage people to call at the house. As you probably know, I'm self-employed and work from home, so I prefer not to be interrupted.'

Or let anyone get too close to Charlotte? Finch wondered. The girl-in-the-tower image seemed even more applicable.

'What about neighbours?' Helen put in.

She was much better than Boyce at picking up the thread of an interview and its unspoken nuances.

'I have no immediate neighbours.' Lambert was a little too quick to make this point and also to add, 'There is one person Charlotte knows quite well. Her name's Jocelyn Harvey. She lives in the village. I can give you her address if you want it.'

It was a diversion and Helen had the sense not to follow it up at length.

'When we leave will do,' she conceded. 'What about school? She must have friends there.'

'Yes, of course she has friends, but the only girl she has any close contact with is Fiona Bradshaw.'

'No boyfriends?'

'Not that I know of,' Lambert replied stiffly. He seemed affronted by the question. 'You'll have to ask at the school. I understand the pupils are very closely monitored by the staff.'

This line of questioning seemed to have been effectively closed by Lambert and Finch took over the interview.

'You said you have no near neighbours,' he remarked, picking up on Lambert's earlier remark. 'As we drove up, I noticed a house a little further along the road.'

'Oh, you mean The Lawns,' Lambert said dismissively, apparently not put out by the question. 'I was speaking of immediate neighbours—people living next door.'

He offered no further information and it was Finch who had to press home the point.

'Who lives there?'

'Someone from London. He's only recently moved into the village. I understand he's leasing the place.'

'Do you know his name?'

Lambert seemed reluctant to reply. It was only after a silence in which Finch raised his eyebrows at him that he continued, 'Noel Murray. Apart from that, I know very little about the man.'

It was obvious Lambert was lying but Finch decided to leave it there for the time being. It might be counterproductive to press him further on the subject. Better perhaps to follow it up during another interview. Besides, time was passing and he was anxious to find out from Stapleton, the inspector in charge of the search, how it was progressing before it was postponed until the following day because of poor light.

Rising to his feet, he held out his hand.

'Thank you for your cooperation, Mr Lambert. I'll be in touch with you again, of course, to let you know how the enquiry's going. By the way, if you're not answering the door to just anybody, may I suggest some sort of code so you'll know it's me? Three slow knocks followed by a couple of quick ones? And while we're on the subject of communicating with one another, do you have an email address? As you're not answering the phone, perhaps I could contact you that way.'

As Lambert searched his pockets for something to write on, Finch obliged by handing him his own pen and a page torn from his notebook.

'Thanks,' Lambert said briefly.

'And while you're writing that down,' Finch continued, 'perhaps you'd add the names and addresses of those people who knew Charlotte fairly well.'

'Yes, of course.' He sounded reluctant but scribbled down the extra information before folding the paper in two and handing it back to Finch, together with the pen.

Ridiculously, the Chief Inspector felt a small buzz of triumph at having got this much out of the man as he pocketed both and, gesturing to Lambert to go ahead, followed him out of the room accompanied by Helen Wyatt.

'Well, what did you make of him?' he asked as they got into the car and set off down the drive towards the gate.

'A strange man,' Helen conceded. She offered the remark tentatively, as if she hadn't yet made up her mind about him. 'He didn't seem to want to tell us anything.'

'Any idea why?'

Before she could reply, they had reached the end of the drive and Finch had to get out to open and close the gate. When he got back in, she glanced briefly in his direction.

'I noticed he hesitated the most when you

105

asked about any near neighbours.'

'So you picked up on that, too. Odd, when you think his only neighbour is just up the road.'

'Could Lambert think the man—Murray, wasn't it—is a possible suspect?'

'Too early to say at this stage. But if he does, wouldn't Lambert be more than anxious to let us know all about him?'

'What about Lambert himself?'

Helen asked the question with apparent innocence but Finch managed to dodge it all the same. He himself had serious reservations about Lambert but he needed time to assimilate the impressions the man had made on him. Discussing them with Helen Wyatt at this stage would be trying to put half-formed ideas into words.

To distract her attention from the topic, he gestured towards the right-hand verge.

'That must be the stop where Charlotte Lambert would have got off the bus, if she'd been on it.'

It was, he estimated, only a couple of minutes' walk from Lambert's house.

'And what's that gateway over there?' he added, pointing this time to the left. They were passing a pair of tall, wire-mesh, security gates on which was hung a board advertising some firm or other. It was impossible to see what lay behind them because of a dense growth of bushes and sapling trees which crowded close.

Helen Wyatt seemed about to draw up but he waved her on.

'Don't stop. We can look at the place another time. I'm anxious to see Murray's first.'

Murray's house was only a short distance further on. By now the car had slowed down to a crawl, giving him plenty of time to observe it, not that there was much to see. A shrubbery hid most of it and all that was visible was a section of a white-painted wall and a glimpse of a porticoed porch with brass carriage lamps on either side. A pair of tall, elaborate, wrought-iron gates closed off the drive from the road, the name, The Lawns, worked into the tracery, one word in each section enclosed in oval cartouches. They put Finch in mind of the embroidered initials on the breast pocket of an expensive dressing-gown.

'Shall I stop?' Helen asked.

Finch shook his head.

'No, keep going. We can call on Murray tomorrow. I'm still curious to know why Lambert was so reluctant to talk about him.'

This time, Helen Wyatt made no attempt to follow up Finch's remark for which the Chief Inspector was silently grateful. Without distraction, he was able to concentrate his attention on the road ahead.

It was an ordinary B country road; no pavements, just wide grass verges on both sides backed by hedges, which were occasionally broken by five-barred gates, allowing glimpses of fields beyond, some cultivated, some pasture, as well as small copses of trees and larger stretches of woodland. Finch regarded these brief, snatched vistas of the landscape with considerable gloom. Searching the area would not be easy. As for witnesses, there were no houses apart from a pair of modest brick and slate cottages built close to the road, which looked deserted although some washing on a line in the garden of the one to the left, together with a child's swing, suggested someone lived there. The garden on the right was empty apart from some bedraggled brussel-sprout stalks and a large, bent crab apple tree, its branches hung with small, bright green fruits, like Christmas lights. The sight of it brought back memories of scrumping crab apples as a child and the sour taste of them in his mouth, which had withered up his tongue.

They were probably tied cottages, Finch concluded, for, a little further on, there was a turning to the left with a green-painted fingerpost announcing Pelham Farm as well as a road sign which read Pelham Lane. The lane, which was narrow and rutted, evidently was little used for tufts of grass were growing up the centre of it, suggesting it merely served as an access route to the farm, which was not visible from the road.

They came upon the search party about fifty yards past the cottages, round an S bend that had hidden them from view until the last moment. About a hundred men were strung out on either side of the road, armed with sticks and billhooks, who were moving slowly and methodically along the verges, parting the long grasses and the creamy froth of cows' parsley and meadowsweet which filled the ditches. Two other groups were working their way across the adjacent fields, the men walking with bent heads as they inspected the ground yard by yard while, a helicopter hovered overhead. It was laborious work, which would probably be quite useless. In the surrounding countryside, there must be hundreds of places where a body could be hidden. The best they could hope for was a lucky find by someone out walking a dog or a pair of lovers looking for somewhere secluded to enjoy what, in Finch's youth, had been known as a bit of necking.

To make matters worse, the light was fading. It was now nearly nine o'clock and the sun was slipping down behind the trees in a great fiery conflagration of red and gold, which underlit the clouds turning them crimson and a sulphurous yellow.

As Finch's car drew to a halt, Inspector Stapleton, who was in charge of the search party, came across to speak to the Chief Inspector through the open passenger window.

His long-chinned, melancholy face, peering in over the edge of the glass, put Finch in mind of an old, sad horse looking down at him from across a fence.

'Any luck?' he asked, although it was obvious from the man's expression that nothing of any use had been found, let alone the missing girl's body.

'Only the usual rubbish,' Stapleton replied. 'It beats me how, whenever we make one of these searches, we always manage to come up with just one shoe; never a pair.'

'Anything on the road itself?'

'Nothing to interest the dogs. They didn't seem to pick up anything worthwhile so they've been packed off back home. And no skid marks to suggest a car stopped or drove off suddenly. No signs of a struggle either.'

'What about the cottages?'

'We've drawn a blank there as well. There's a married couple in the left-hand one but both were out at the relevant time. The husband works at Pelham Farm, up the lane, and the wife had gone into Chelmsford on the bus with the kids. Or so the old boy who lives in the other cottage told us. He's retired and a bit deaf. He spent the afternoon in the back room watching telly with the sound turned up so he heard nothing; no car; no screams. Same with the farm up the lane. It's too far from the road for anyone to have seen or heard anything but I sent Sergeant Greenstock up there to make enquiries, just in case. He'll be writing up a report but it's going to be another dead loss, I'm afraid.'

Given the circumstances, it was an unfortunate choice of words; not that Stapleton seemed aware of it. There was not a flicker of humour or apology in his voice or expression.

'Well, keep up the good work,' Finch replied with forced cheerfulness. That was not a happy choice of phrase either and he was relieved to give Helen Wyatt a nod to tell her to drive on.

'Where to now?' she asked. 'Back the way we came?'

'No; go on. I want to see the whole of the route she took from the point where she caught the bus in Foxton to where it broke down.'

This last part of her journey finished a couple of hundred yards further on at two bus stops, one on each side of the road. A second sign, another green-painted fingerpost marked Hoe Green, pointed to a turning to the right which presumably led to the village.

Leaving the Sergeant at the wheel, Finch got out of the car and stood for a moment on the verge, looking about him.

God knows what he hoped to see. The place was indistinguishable from any other stretch of the road, apart from the lay-bys for the buses to draw into and a couple of litter bins lined up next to the bus stops. In the distance, he

111

caught a glimpse of the top of a church tower poking above the trees marking the position of Hoe Green village, he assumed.

The police vehicles that had brought the search party from Chelmsford were parked along one side of the road with a uniformed constable in charge of them. Recognising Finch, he saluted, a courtesy that the Chief Inspector acknowledged by briefly ducking his head. Despite his years in the force, he still found this deference to rank something of an embarrassment. All the same, the mark of respect seemed to have brisked him up for he was in a better mood as he clambered back into the car.

'Keep going,' he said.

'To Foxton?' Helen Wyatt asked.

It was the place where Charlotte Lambert had caught the bus.

Finch nodded before continuing in a musing voice, as if speaking to himself, 'At some point, we're going to have to set up a reconstruction of the girl's journey home, including her walk along that last stretch of road. I'll speak to the Chief Super about it. We could combine it with a TV appeal for witnesses. Sanderson can head that up as well. He's got more of a telly personality than I have,' and here he gave a small, self-deprecating grin, 'as well as a posher voice.'

The road continued in its rambling fashion between the verges and the boundary hedges.

Through the open windows the sweet scent of the countryside filled the car, the air already cooling as the evening drew on and the shadows of the trees lengthened. It would soon be lighting-up time.

Foxton was a further mile and a half along the road, which ended in a T-junction where it divided, the left-hand turning leading on to Banfield, the one on the right continuing for a couple of hundred yards before joining a new extension of the by-pass, which eventually led to Chelmsford and on to Colchester, and which, according to the information given to him by Sergeant Bridger, had its own separate bus service, the 176.

As Bridger had also described, the bus stop stood a little to the left of the T-junction, a more elaborate structure than the simple, white-painted metal poles that marked the stops along the Northorpe–Foxton road. This one even had a shelter with a bench and a litter bin. Timetables for the two bus services, the 143 and the 176, were displayed on a board fastened to the side of the shelter. A few yards from it was the Bradshaws' house, again as Bridger had described.

Helen Wyatt slowed down and looked enquiringly at Finch but he waved her on. There was no need to stop. He'd be back the following day to interview the Bradshaws, when he could look about as much as he wanted at his leisure. The brief glimpse he caught of the house—detached 1930s with fake beams tacked on to the upper façade— was enough for the moment. He paid more attention to the bus stop.

The car turned right towards Chelmsford and a little further on came to the dual carriageway of the by-pass, where it picked up speed. They'd be back at Divisional Headquarters before lighting-up time.

CHAPTER TWO

Friday, 18th July.

It's been over a week since I last made an entry in my journal. That was on Sunday, 6th July, when Charlotte was here for the weekend and we went to Suffolk and stayed at Aldeburgh. The last sentence I wrote after that weekend describes how she took my arm and hugged it close to her side: 'And so we walked together, the two of us, and I thought I hadn't been so happy for a long, long time.'

Rereading that sentence this evening, I could remember that moment so clearly—the taste of salt on my lips and the harsh cries of the gulls as they swooped and dived over the estuary. And the warmth of Charlotte's arm against mine, although that part of the memory is so painful that I've had to force it to one side and think instead of the impeccable blue of the sky and the hard glitter of the sun on the sea.

People speak so glibly about their hearts breaking but, as I've learnt today, that is not an exaggeration. The sense of loss is unbearable, a great, aching void inside the chest that pulsates and shrieks silently with pain; the same feeling I had when my father told me my mother had left us. The only passage that comes anywhere near describing that agony is

115

in Shakespeare's play *King John*:
> '*Grief fills the room up of my absent child,*
> *Lies in his bed, walks up and down with*
> *me . . .*'

I remember the English master at that boys' boarding school in Suffolk quoting those lines when he was giving us a talk about Shakespeare's life and how it's believed they refer to the death of Hamnet, his only son, who was eleven years old.

Those words came back to me so vividly this afternoon after Finch and his sergeant had left, and I went upstairs to Charlotte's bedroom. I think in a crazy way that I was looking for her. But she wasn't there, of course. Her books were and her drawings and her scruffy, one-eared toy rabbit which her mother had given her when she was two was still sitting on the bed. But no Charlotte.

I took the vase of roses I'd left on her dressing-table as a welcome-home present and scattered them in the garden.

Charlotte is dead. She disappeared on the way home from the Bradshaws' this afternoon and I knew at once from the expression on Finch's face that there isn't any hope she's still alive, although he didn't say so. He called at the house late this afternoon with a woman police officer to speak to me about Charlotte's disappearance. Or rather her abduction, because that's what he seems to think has happened to her.

She was walking home from Hoe Green because the bus had broken down. She hasn't been seen since. Somewhere along that stretch of road she was abducted by someone in a car. It's the only rational explanation. And it had to be by someone she knew. She wouldn't have accepted a lift from a stranger.

Finch told me the police are searching the fields along the Foxton road but so far have found nothing, and I don't really expect they will. If she's dead, as I believe she is, there are acres of fields and woods near the village where her body could be hidden.

I keep getting flashing images of her lying in long grass, her face turned up to the sky. Ridiculous, isn't it? But I've read somewhere about a condition—Post-Traumatic Stress Disorder—in which people who've experienced a trauma have brief after-images of the car-crash or the fire in which they were involved. In my case, they're entirely imaginary but so vivid and detailed they could be real.

Among them is one that is real, that of Murray's expression that afternoon when he called here to return the file on Northorpe Hall and was aware of Charlotte watching his lips. It was a look of raw, sexual desire which made it quite clear that he lusted after her— her beauty, her innocence, her virginity.

So I know without any doubt that it's Murray who's abducted her. Apart from the memory of his expression that day, he fits all the criteria. He knew Charlotte; he has a car; he lives nearby so that offering her a lift would seem perfectly natural.

I can picture quite clearly what happened—Charlotte walking along the Foxton road under the trees, Murray's car drawing up alongside, Charlotte getting into the passenger seat.

I haven't got the courage yet to picture what happened after that but it's a common enough scenario.

I decided not to tell Finch any of this when he called today. Some instinct which I didn't stop to rationalise, told me to keep silent. Thinking about it now, I understand why.

Firstly, I haven't much confidence in Finch's ability as a policeman. He's a quiet man, observant and probably shrewd, but he doesn't give an impression of decisiveness or action. Part of this is caused by his faint Essex accent, not obtrusive, but it makes me think he's not very sophisticated and wouldn't be a match intellectually for Murray. I may be doing the man an injustice but I daren't risk confiding in him my conviction of Murray's guilt only to find that Finch has bungled the investigation and the man gets off scot-free.

There's also the law to consider. Even if Murray is taken to court and found guilty, he'd be sentenced to life imprisonment, which usually means fifteen years; that's all. With good conduct he could be out in under ten.

I'm not prepared to risk that. I'll bring the man to justice myself; though quite how, I haven't yet decided.

CHAPTER THREE

Finch and Helen Wyatt returned to Foxton the following morning, approaching it this time by the direct route from Chelmsford, along the by-pass, instead of through the village of Northorpe.

It was a deliberate choice on Finch's part. After interviewing the Bradshaws, he intended going back to Northorpe to question Murray, Alex Lambert's neighbour, at the same time checking with Stapleton how the search was going. He had already agreed with Stapleton that, once the road into the village had been fully examined, the fields surrounding Lambert's house as well as Murray's and any outbuildings should also be searched on the principle that, if the girl had not been abducted by a stranger and her body taken miles away, the most likely scenario, and one which the Chief Inspector tended to prefer, was that she had been offered a lift by someone she knew and that her killer had disposed of her body much nearer home.

Murray seemed a possible suspect. So, too, did Lambert himself. Now that he had had time to go over in his mind his interview with Lambert the previous day, he had come to the conclusion that his initial misgivings about the man and his relationship with his daughter were justified. There was something distinctly odd, he felt, about the whole set up: the isolated house, the drawn blinds, the lack of neighbours. Lambert was also an unusual character, as isolated as the house he lived in. Even the drawn blinds had their own significance. As a precaution against prying eyes, they were understandable. Lambert preferred to keep his grief private. Finch could sympathise with that. Under similar circumstances, he, too, might have wanted to shut out the world. But he had a strong intuitive feeling that the drawn blinds were only the outward manifestation on Lambert's part of a need to shut out everybody and everything, as an animal will go to ground when it's injured or in shock and, if that were true, he wondered who or what in the past had traumatised Lambert so deeply. He was certainly damaged in some way, Finch believed.

They went first to the Bradshaws' house, where Finch was hoping to speak to Derek Bradshaw as well as his wife, Pauline. But as Helen Wyatt was parking in the drive behind a shabby, dark blue Ford Fiesta, the front door abruptly opened and a man, Bradshaw himself, Finch assumed, came out, struggling to put on his jacket.

He was a stocky man in his forties, with blunt features bunched together and sandy hair, which was already receding and turning grey. Judging by the frown lines between his eyebrows, so deep they seemed to have been gouged out of the flesh, he was morose by nature and a congenital worrier. He certainly looked very put out by the presence of Finch's car.

'Who are you? What do you want?' he demanded, bending down at the open passenger's window.

'Detective Chief Inspector Finch and Detective Sergeant Wyatt,' Finch replied in a conciliatory tone, flashing his ID card.

Bradshaw climbed down a little.

'Sorry,' he mumbled. 'I suppose you've come about . . .'

His voice trailed away as if he were reluctant to put into words the reason for their visit. It was a natural unwillingness. In his career as a policeman, Finch had come across it on many occasions, as if murder, or in this case suspected abduction followed by murder, was a taboo subject not to be referred to out loud.

Finch completed the sentence for him.

'About Charlotte Lambert's disappearance? Yes, that's why we're here. We'd like to ask you a few questions.'

'I can't tell you anything,' Bradshaw replied. 'I wasn't here yesterday. I was at the shop. You'll need to talk to my wife. And I can't stop now anyway. I'm expecting a delivery at nine o'clock sharp. Could you move your car so I can get mine out?'

Finch nodded and Helen Wyatt backed the car a few yards down the drive to a place where it was wide enough to allow both cars to pass one another. As he drew alongside, Bradshaw lowered his window.

'Listen!' he said urgently. 'My daughter's home. I don't want her harassed. She knows about Charlotte and she's upset enough as it is.'

His manner was not exactly hostile but it certainly wasn't very amicable either and it struck Finch that the man had few social skills.

'Of course. I understand . . .' Finch began but before he had time to finish, Bradshaw had driven off in a flurry of gravel spurting out from under his back wheels.

He and Helen exchanged glances at this display of bad-tempered driving prompted by who knew what. Impatience? Dislike of the police? Anxiety of being late for the delivery he had spoken of? Whatever the cause, it had been witnessed by a woman who had followed Bradshaw out of the front door and who stepped forward apologetically as Helen eased the car further up the drive and drew up outside the house.

'Mrs Bradshaw?' Finch asked, getting out of the car and approaching her.

A pleasant woman with plump, plain features, she had a naive, almost childlike appeal about her and was clearly flustered by her husband's behaviour.

'You mustn't take too much notice of Derek,' she said hurriedly. 'This dreadful business with Charlotte has upset him, like it has all of us, and he's up to his ears in work as well. To be frank, we shouldn't have moved here. He had a good job in London and he's not that keen on the country.'

Her need to confide in someone, anyone, suggested she, too, wasn't content with her present life and that her husband almost certainly failed to supply her with the affection and sympathy she obviously craved. With a glance back over her shoulder at the house, she added, lowering her voice, 'Will you need to question Fiona? Derek and I have already told her about Charlotte. We thought it best to let her know the truth straight away so she'll have the weekend to come to terms with it before she goes back to school.'

It was Helen, thank God, who answered her. Finch had never been any good at dealing with distress, especially in a woman.

'Don't worry, Mrs Bradshaw,' she told her. 'We'll send along a couple of officers this afternoon who are specially trained in interviewing children. But we'll have to ask her some questions. You understand?'

Mrs Bradshaw nodded, looking faintly relieved, and gestured to them to follow her into the house.

'Wait in here a moment,' she went on,

opening a door on the right. 'I'll tell Fiona to stay in the garden until you've gone.'

The room into which she showed them was evidently the family living room. It was shabby and untidy with books and papers strewn about and photographs on nearly every flat surface. A tabby cat lay asleep on one of the armchairs. Through the french windows, which overlooked the back garden, they could see Mrs Bradshaw rapidly signing to a young girl with her father's sandy hair, who was sitting on a swing. The urgency of the hand signals and the manner in which the girl turned her head to look towards the house made it clear what message Mrs Bradshaw was conveying. As she finished, the girl got off the swing and began to walk slowly away up the garden, head hanging and shoulders bent, a personification of grief and loss.

A few moments later, Mrs Bradshaw came into the room looking flushed and blinking back tears.

'She's going to miss Charlotte so much,' she said. 'She's her best friend. I suppose there's no news?'

'Not yet,' he replied gravely. 'But it's early days.'

Mrs Bradshaw said nothing but the expression on her face suggested that she had no great hope of the girl being found alive. It was a quality Finch had noticed before in certain women—not exactly a hardness but a capacity to face reality with a quiet stoicism.

He said, 'I know you've already given a statement to Sergeant Bridger, Mrs Bradshaw, but there are one or two points I'd like you to expand on a little. You said you saw Charlotte waiting at the bus stop. Where exactly were you standing?'

'On the doorstep,' she replied without any hesitation. 'I'd just gone with her to the door to say goodbye and I stayed there until the bus came. I do it every time she comes—I mean, came.' For a moment, her control faltered. 'You can see the heads and shoulders of anyone at the bus stop over the top of the hedge. Not all of them; only the top half.'

It was a minor point but she seemed to need this scrupulous attention to the truth, as if even the smallest detail might be crucial to the success of the investigation.

'Was anyone else waiting?'

'No; only Charlotte.'

'I believe she caught the same bus, the 143, to Northorpe at 4.25 every other Friday afternoon. Have you ever seen anyone else catching that bus? Or hanging about the bus stop at about that time?'

'No; no one.'

She sounded quite positive.

Helen Wyatt took over the questioning.

'How many people might have known Charlotte was in the habit of catching that bus?'

Mrs Bradshaw considered the question for several moments, her plump features crumpled with anxious concentration.

'I don't really know,' she said at last. 'You see, we're at the far end of the village. Most of the people live further down the road and would get on the bus at the stop outside the post office. I can't tell you how many of those would catch that particular bus. Not many, I would imagine. It's a bit late for people to go into Chelmsford shopping and, if they did, they'd catch the other bus, the 176, which goes along the by-pass. The 143 goes all round the villages and takes much longer. You'd do better to ask at the post office. The lady in there could probably tell you.'

'Thank you. We'll certainly speak to her,' Helen said. 'What about other friends Charlotte had apart from Fiona? Did Charlotte mention anyone in particular?'

'Not that I know of,' Mrs Bradshaw replied and glanced involuntarily towards the window overlooking the garden, where her daughter had resumed her seat on the swing and was rocking it backwards and forwards in a listless manner with one foot on the ground.

Turning back to them, her face even more drawn, she expressed the same concern her husband had voiced.

'I know you'll have to question her but I don't want her upset.'

'There's no fear of that,' Finch told her and

127

repeated Helen Wyatt's reassurance about the specially trained police officers.

They left shortly afterwards, Finch remarking as they got into the car, 'I'll get Stapleton to organise house-to-house enquiries in Foxton as well as Northorpe. God knows how long that will take.'

He seemed daunted by the prospect of the task ahead and the number of man-hours it would involve.

They set off in the direction of Northorpe, taking in reverse the same route they'd followed the day before and along which the 143 bus had also travelled with Charlotte Lambert on board. Passing Hoe Green, where the bus had broken down and the girl had set off on foot, Helen Wyatt slowed down at the sight of a woman standing at the bus stop, holding a toddler by the hand. But Finch waved her on. He'd make sure Stapleton included Hoe Green in his door-to-door enquiries, in which the woman would be routinely questioned about her movements at the time of Charlotte Lambert's disappearance.

'I want to interview Murray,' he said by way of explanation. 'After the Bradshaws, he's top of the list of people to see this morning.'

Murray was at home. His silver Audi stood outside the pillared portico they had so far only glimpsed. Seen at closer quarters and without the barrier of trees and shrubbery, the house looked imposing. It was what in estate agent's jargon is known as a 'des res'. Finch's first reaction was to wonder how Murray managed to afford what was almost certainly an expensive lease on the property and concluded he must be doing well for himself. There was indeed an air of money and success about the man when he opened the front door to them; nothing flashy; Murray had better taste than to flaunt his wealth, but there was no disguising the quality and likely cost of the casual linen slacks and shirt he was wearing, nor the gold bracelet of his watch, just visible below the left-hand cuff. Money and success had also given him that sheen which Finch had noticed before on wealthy people, that subtle gloss on hair and skin and teeth, which added an extra polish to the man's good looks.

He was pleasant, affable and apparently unfazed by their arrival at his front door, stepping aside to welcome them inside the house with a friendly gesture before shepherding them into a large drawing room, a little too pink and plush for Finch's liking and not to Murray's either, it seemed, for he directed an amused grimace at them as he invited them to sit down.

Finch was immediately aware of the man's charm and the gift he had of making even strangers feel immediately at ease. At the same time, he wondered how genuine it was.

129

Not very, he decided. Probably like his good looks, it wasn't much more than skin deep. For some reason, the thought cheered him up considerably.

He and Helen Wyatt sat down side by side on one of a pair of large sofas covered in raspberry red leather, which sighed voluptuously under their weight. Murray took a smaller club chair which had its back to the patio doors, hung with heavily swagged and fringed velvet curtains, and giving a view of a garden which consisted, it seemed, almost entirely of lawn.

It was Murray, of course, who opened the interview. He had a natural gift for taking centre stage.

'I assume you've come about Charlotte Lambert's disappearance. What a dreadful business!' he began, his expression suitably sombre. 'Is there any news yet?'

It was the usual question to which Finch gave the usual answer.

'Not yet, I'm afraid,' he said before leaning back into the sofa, inviting Murray to continue.

He was quite content to let the man direct proceedings. In his experience, people like him, articulate, self-confident, used to being in charge, were more likely to divulge more than they intended in an open, informal interview than they would be in a more controlled question-and-answer session.

Cocking his head encouragingly to one side, he waited for Murray to continue.

'Such a shock!' he went on. 'God knows what Alex must be suffering. I've tried ringing him but it seems he's disconnected the phone. Not that I blame him. If I were in his shoes, I wouldn't want people ringing me up to commiserate. It's such an awful tragedy! The girl's deaf—I assume you know that?—and so young and pretty! A dreadful, dreadful loss!'

'You've met her?' Finch asked.

'Only the once.'

Murray answered a little too quickly, as if anxious to get that fact established straight away.

'Here?'

Finch cocked his head again.

'Oh, heavens no! At Lambert's house. It was a couple of weeks ago. I called to return some information he'd lent me.' When Finch remained silent, head still to one side, Murray continued, 'It was about Northorpe Hall. Eighteenth century, or so it said. As a matter of fact, it's just down the road from here. It's a ruin now but evidently it was a superb place in its heyday.'

'Indeed!' Finch said pleasantly and again fell silent, wondering what Murray was trying to cover up with this little flourish of words which, like a stage magician's patter, was designed, he felt, to divert his attention from some other more important aspect of the

131

situation.

On cue, Helen Wyatt picked up the questioning.

'You understand, Mr Murray, that we're interviewing everyone who knew Charlotte Lambert and who might have offered her a lift home yesterday afternoon along the Foxton road. Do you mind telling me what you were doing between quarter past four and five o'clock?'

'Of course I don't mind! I'm delighted to help in any way I can. Between quarter past four and five, you said? Let me see. I think I was at Mrs Gunter's about that time.'

'Mrs Gunter's?' Finch put in. He remembered the name from the list Lambert had given him the day before of local people who knew his daughter.

'She's an elderly lady who lives in the village. Hers is the detached Regency house, the Old Rectory. It's on the left-hand side of the road as you drive into the village from here. I'd arranged to meet her at about three o'clock.'

Again there was a small silence and Murray, who seemed uncharacteristically flustered by these short breaks in the proceedings, hastened to fill the gap.

'She'd heard I was a financial adviser. She asked me to call to discuss her investments.'

'And at what time did you leave?' Again it was Helen who took over the interview.

Murray hesitated, covering up his indecision with a little laugh.

'Quite honestly, I don't know. I wasn't looking at the time. She's a charming lady and we were chatting away like old friends.'

'Mrs Gunter might remember?' Helen suggested.

'She may indeed. But let me think.' He waited for a moment, putting his knuckles to his forehead in the manner of Rodin's sculpture, *The Thinker*, before continuing, 'It must have been about quarter to five.'

It was Finch's turn to pick up the questioning, a technique which the two of them had perfected between them. Like a spectator at a tennis match, Murray's head swivelled to the left and right as they passed the interview to and fro between them.

'And what did you do after you'd left Mrs Gunter's?'

'I drove over to see Jocelyn Harvey.'

It was another name on Lambert's list.

'At her house?' Helen Wyatt put in.

'No; at her shop. She has a boutique in Chelmsford.'

'What route did you take, Mr Murray?'

Finch asked the question with apparent casualness, giving it no more weight than any of the other queries but Murray was immediately on the defensive.

'I didn't go along the Foxton road, if that's what you're suggesting,' he snapped back, dropping the mask of genial cooperation.

'I wasn't suggesting anything of the kind,' Finch replied equably. 'As you probably know, there are two routes into Chelmsford, either via Foxton and then along the by-pass or, alternatively, through Nettleden, which takes you to the by-pass at Church End, a few miles further on.'

'I'm perfectly well aware of that,' Murray said. He had recovered some of his composure but was still on the defensive. 'I went along the Nettleden road. It's nearer to Mrs Gunter's house and saved me having to drive through the village.'

'What time did you arrive at Mrs Harvey's shop?' Helen put in, her voice and manner calm and pleasant.

Murray answered too quickly.

'I have no idea. I'm not one of those people who keep checking on my watch every five minutes. Ask Jocelyn. She may remember. As for the time I left, if it's any use to your enquiry, she closed the shop at half past five or thereabouts. Then she had to empty the till, put the cash and cheques into the safe and get herself ready to leave. We drove back to Northorpe, taking both cars, and stopped at the Red Lion in Nettleden on the way for a drink and a meal. I got back here about ten o'clock because I remember catching the beginning of the news on BBC One.'

'Thank you, Mr Murray. You've been most

cooperative,' Finch said, rising to his feet. His voice and expression were perfectly serious and it was impossible to tell whether or not he was being ironic.

'I bet the first thing he does is to phone Mrs Harvey to warn her of our visit,' he continued a little later when, having said goodbye, he and Helen drove away from the house.

' "Warn"?' Helen repeated, raising her eyebrows.

'Well, put her in the picture then,' Finch said, modifying his statement.

'You don't like him very much, do you?'

Finch made an impatient movement with his shoulders.

'Like. Dislike. It doesn't matter. I simply feel he's not trustworthy.'

'The charm certainly began to slip a little,' Helen remarked. 'Depending on the timing, he could, of course, have driven to Chelmsford along the Foxton road and met Charlotte on the way. As for getting rid of the body, he could've put it in the boot of his car and dumped it later, after he'd returned to Northorpe. He'd have all night for that.'

Finch merely grunted in reply. Although Helen's comments made sense, he was still not disposed to discussing the case so early in the investigation. But he made up his mind to get DC Kyle to check Murray's name in the National Police Register, just in case. He was

135

about to tell Helen of his decision when his attention was diverted.

'Pull up here for a moment,' he said.

As the car drew up on the right-hand verge, Finch got out and, calling back over his shoulder, 'I shan't be long!', he crossed over the road to where an opening in the hedge was barricaded off by the pair of high security mesh gates which he had noticed the day before on his way back from Lambert's house. The gates were padlocked and, after testing that they were secure by rattling them a couple of times, he peered through the mesh. There was some sort of driveway on the other side, almost lost beneath the trees and bushes that crowded the site although the remains of the brick pillars of a once imposing gateway were still standing. Of the house itself, or rather its ruins, nothing was visible through the dense foliage.

A board fastened to one of the gates announced that trespassers would be prosecuted together with the additional warning: DANGER! KEEP OUT! Below was a smaller sign giving the name, address and telephone number of the security firm in charge of the place.

Having quickly jotted down these details in his notebook, Finch glanced up and down the road. Although neither Lambert's nor Murray's houses could be seen, apart from the gateway to The Lawns and a small window in the gable end at Field Lodge, it was obvious both houses were only a short distance from Northorpe Hall, which he assumed this place must be. Whether or not there was another access to the grounds at the back of the site was something he could leave Stapleton to investigate. What interested Finch was the realisation that, if you had a body to get rid of, here was a good place to hide it.

Satisfied, he got back into the car and told Helen Wyatt to drive on but to stop again at Lambert's house.

He himself wasn't quite sure why he came to this decision. It was partly the need to let Lambert know the search was being extended into the village but he had the feeling this was only an excuse. He wanted to see how the man was coping, not out of malice, nor from a genuine feeling of sympathy for him either. It was more an urge to simply observe Lambert again, perhaps even to rattle his cage a little, but mostly to find out more about his relationship with Murray.

Why had Lambert seemed reluctant to involve Murray in the police enquiry? Lambert was intelligent. It must have occurred to him that Murray would be a likely suspect. He'd met the girl; he was a near neighbour; he more convincingly fulfilled the requirements for a likely candidate from whom Charlotte Lambert might have accepted a lift than a putative passing stranger.

They were not Lambert's only visitors apparently. Someone had already called at Field Lodge before them, for a large bunch of roses and carnations, elaborately wrapped in cellophane and decorated with ribbon streamers, was propped up against the front door.

Helen stooped to pick it up and examine the little gift tag that was attached to it. Without speaking, she turned it so that Finch could see what was written on it. It read: *To Alex. My thoughts are with you all the time. Love Jocelyn.*

Finch pulled a wry face. Judging by the look of them, the flowers had been lying there for several hours. Then, turning to the door, he knocked, using the signal he had agreed with Lambert.

For several long moments nothing happened.

'Perhaps he's gone out,' Helen suggested.

'No; he's at home,' Finch assured her. He didn't add that Lambert would no more leave the sanctuary of the house than a sick animal would venture out of its refuge into open country.

Seconds later, the door was opened and Lambert appeared on the threshold.

'These were left on the doorstep,' Helen explained, holding out the bouquet.

Lambert took it reluctantly, glancing about him as if unsure what to do with it, before standing aside to let them come into the hall where he dumped it on a small telephone table.

I bet they finish up in the bin, Finch thought to himself.

Without speaking, Lambert showed them into the room where they'd met before. The blinds were still drawn and, in the creamy twilight, Lambert looked more ghastly than he had on that first occasion. His clothes were creased, as if he'd slept in them, and his hair had not been combed. He even seemed to have lost weight. Finch was shocked to see how quickly he had deteriorated.

Although he felt a twinge of pity for the man, the detective in him wondered what had caused this sudden decline. Grief and despair at the loss of his daughter had obviously played a major part. But was guilt also to blame?

He said, 'I thought I'd better let you know, Mr Lambert, that the search is going to be widened today to take in the village and the surrounding area, including any outbuildings, so I'd be grateful if your garage and any sheds are left unlocked until the search is over. We're also starting house-to-house enquiries. So if you see any police officers about the village or they call here, that's what it's all about. By the way, one of the places they'll be searching is the grounds of Northorpe Hall. I believe you're familiar with them?'

He made the question sound casual, a mere

conversational make-weight, but he watched Lambert's face closely for a reaction.

'Yes; I have been there,' Lambert replied after a long hesitation.

'So, in spite of the security gates, there is a way in?'

'At the back,' Lambert said shortly. 'There's a gap in the fencing.'

'Ah, right!'

Finch looked pleased as if the answer had proved something to his satisfaction.

There was another silence in which Lambert turned towards the door, suggesting that, as far as he was concerned, the interview was over. Finch failed to pick up the hint.

'I was thinking,' he continued in the same pleasant, conversational style, 'that I'd look round the place myself. As a matter of fact, Mr Murray mentioned it when I called on him earlier this morning. It sounds interesting. How old is it?'

'I'm not sure. Eighteenth century, I believe,' Lambert said curtly. His impatience to get rid of them was obvious.

Finch nodded and made for the door. He'd got what he came for. Lambert had lied. According to Murray, Lambert had lent him a folder of information about Northorpe Hall, which included the date of the building. As Murray had no reason to lie about this particular point, Finch could only conclude that Lambert was trying to disassociate himself from either any contact with Murray or knowledge of Northorpe Hall. Or perhaps both.

Whatever the reason, the Chief Inspector walked back to the car, well pleased with the outcome of the visit.

CHAPTER FOUR

Saturday, 19th July.

Damn! Damn! Damn! Finch and his Sergeant have just left, their visit ostensibly, according to Finch, to let me know that the search is going to be extended into the village. But I think he had an ulterior motive, quite what I'm not sure. He seemed to go out of his way to mention M and the fact that M had spoken of Northorpe Hall.

I don't know quite what to make of Finch's interview with M and what it's leading up to. I wish I had control over the enquiry and the way in which it develops regarding M. But of course, I know that's out of the question. Realistically speaking, M is going to be a suspect in the eyes of the police anyway. He lives nearby; he knew Charlotte; he's self-employed so he's free to come and go as he likes. If I were the police and knew nothing of that meeting he had with Charlotte, he'd be on my list of suspects all the same.

I'm also uncertain why Finch should be so interested in Northorpe Hall, unless as a likely hiding-place for Charlotte's body. I suppose that, too, is possible, and it certainly fits in with the sequence of events that, now that I'm over the first dreadful shock of her disappearance, I can envisage calmly and I'm convinced took place. M is driving along the Foxton road, sees Charlotte and offers her a lift home. But instead of bringing her here, he makes some excuse to turn into the drive of The Lawns, persuades her inside and kills her when she tries to fend off his advances.

Left with her body, he has to decide what to do with it and Northorpe Hall seems the logical place to hide it. It's close by his house; it's overgrown and offers plenty of places where a body could be hidden; it's not open to the public, unlike a field or a wood where anyone out walking might stumble across it.

I assume the police will search it themselves at some time; possibly today. I could keep watch on what they're doing from the attic window, which overlooks Northorpe Hall, or at least the stretch of road that leads up to its entrance. But whether they do or not, I'll search the grounds myself later tonight, just to make sure there's no sign that M used the place to hide Charlotte's body.

Oh, God! Is there no end to the torment? If he had left her body there, it would be a form of sacrilege, like desecrating a church with satanic rites. It's a place of such peace and beauty which I've always associated with Charlotte, especially the grotto. I feel the whole place would be made unclean. God damn him to hell.

11.30 p.m.

I've just finished rereading this entry and realised I've started referring to Murray as M; not that it matters. The same letter can apply just as well to one as to the other. They are alike in so many ways and both are guilty of causing the death of the two people who I loved more than anyone else in the world.

CHAPTER FIVE

As Murray had described it, the Old Rectory was directly opposite the church and a little distance from the new rectory, built to replace it in the Sixties, an ugly square building of red brick and tile with double-glazed windows and a large gravelled forecourt big enough to hold several cars if need be. It was functional and charmless.

In comparison, the Old Rectory, a Regency house, had grace and character but probably lacked the necessary amenities. The sash windows might be elegant, the porch with its pagoda style roof and slender cast-iron supports graceful, the fanlight over the front door delightful in its pattern of interlocking semi-circles, but there was hardly room to park even one car let alone those of the members of the various committees and subcommittees for fund-raising or flower-arranging rotas without which a church nowadays could hardly function satisfactorily.

Mrs Gunter, Finch was told, was in the back garden, and he and Helen were conducted through a cool, dim hall smelling of flowers and furniture polish into the dazzling sunlight by a young housekeeper wearing a tabard-style overall, such as some air hostesses wear when serving meals.

Mrs Gunter was lying in the shade of a lilac tree on a garden recliner, propped up on blue and white checked cushions that matched the pattern of the mattress on the chair, spectacles on nose, book on lap, a jug of orange juice and a glass at hand on a little table, covered with a cloth of the same fabric. Two smaller upright chairs, cushioned in matching gingham, stood nearby, making up the set.

Closing her book and removing her glasses, Mrs Gunter watched their progress across the lawn with undisguised interest.

'Detective Chief Inspector Finch and Detective Sergeant Wyatt,' the housekeeper announced solemnly in what sounded to Finch like an east European accent. Polish, perhaps? Or possibly Hungarian?

'Thank you, Maria,' Mrs Gunter said graciously. 'Would you please bring coffee for us?' Turning to Finch and Helen, she continued, 'Do sit down. I assume you're here about Charlotte Lambert's disappearance. Such a ghastly business! Now, is there anything I can do to help?'

The chairs were so placed that Mrs Gunter's recliner dominated the semi-circle, not an arrangement that Finch would have chosen, for it placed Mrs Gunter too much centre-stage for his liking. It was a position she was evidently used to for she showed no unease at being the focus of attention; rather the opposite, in fact.

146

She was, Finch guessed, in her seventies although it was difficult to gauge her exact age. She was wearing a stylish broad-brimmed straw hat, which cast a shadow over her face although, from what he could see of her features, she was still a handsome, well-preserved woman with bright, intelligent eyes and a touch of humour about her carefully painted pink lips. The dress she was wearing, the same shade as the lipstick, was a long gown-like garment, a kaftan perhaps—Finch wasn't very knowledgeable about women's clothes—and her pretty little feet with their high, arched insteps were thrust into white sandals. Observing them, Finch recalled a piece of schoolboy folklore current when he was an adolescent: that women with high insteps were good in bed. In Mrs Gunter's case, he could believe it. She looked as if she had been something of a 'goer' as she reclined there against the gingham cushions, a study in pink and white and blue, a colour scheme she must have chosen for her own benefit as she couldn't have known the police would call on her at that particular time.

'Yes, we're here about Charlotte Lambert,' Finch agreed. 'We're checking on everyone who knows her and might be able to help with our enquiries. You've met her, I believe?'

'Not often; at most three or four times in the village. Her father seems to want to protect her from other people, perhaps

147

because of her deafness. You realise she's profoundly deaf?'

'Yes, I do,' Finch replied.

He was interested to learn that Mrs Gunter confirmed his own suspicions: that Lambert was too possessive of his daughter.

'It's understandable, of course,' Mrs Gunter was continuing. 'She's such a very pretty girl. Quite exquisite. She has that other-worldly air about her which I've noticed deaf people often have. I would imagine some boys find her quite irresistible.'

Finch sat back, letting her run on. There were specific questions he wanted to ask her but they could wait. Mrs Gunter was evidently a shrewd and observant woman, particularly where relationships between men and women were concerned, an interest that was no doubt based on her own experiences when younger. As he'd already guessed, she would have been exquisite herself and used to attracting male attention. Although those days were over, it still gave her pleasure and amusement to watch younger people taking part in the sort of flirtatious games at which she had once been so expert a player.

'Do you know of anyone in particular who is interested in her?' Finch asked. He was beginning to find the necessity of having to use the present tense when referring to Charlotte as if she were still alive not only mendacious but difficult to maintain.

'I suppose you mean in the village?' Mrs Gunter replied. 'No; there's not anyone in particular that I know of. When she's seen about the place, it's generally in the post office or the shop, not the most likely venues for a romantic encounter. And, of course, her father is always with her. I'm afraid I can't be more specific than that.'

It was interesting to note that, as she spoke, Mrs Gunter put on her tinted reading glasses which had been lying in her lap with her discarded book. It was a significant gesture designed to hide her eyes from Finch's scrutiny. So, he concluded, she probably did know of certain local male inhabitants who were attracted to Charlotte Lambert but preferred not to name them, although he thought he could guess the type of man she had in mind—middle class, like herself, getting on in age, respectable, who would not wish to be thought of as lusting after a fourteen-year-old schoolgirl.

As if she had read his thoughts, Mrs Gunter took off the sunglasses and added firmly, 'There is no one I know of who is capable of abducting that girl. Or of murdering her. Because that's why you're here, isn't it, Chief Inspector? It's not just about a disappearance; it's a case of murder.'

It was a clever move on her part because it shifted the focus of the interview away from herself and on to Finch. But he refused to be drawn.

'We have no proof of that, Mrs Gunter.'

She had the grace to look chastened.

'Of course. And let us hope she's found safe and well. Now, if there's anything I can do to help . . .'

She left the rest of the sentence dangling in mid-air, as if expecting Finch to use the opportunity to bring the interview to a close. But so far, he hadn't reached the purpose of his visit.

Speaking casually, he said, 'I understand Mr Murray called on you yesterday afternoon? I believe you wanted to discuss your finances with him.'

Interestingly, she did not put on her sunglasses on this occasion, although one hand went out to touch them as they lay in her lap. Instead, she looked straight at Finch and then asked, holding his gaze:

'Were those his exact words—that I asked him to advise me on my finances?'

'Yes, they were, Mrs Gunter; word for word.'

'Then I'm afraid you've been misled, Chief Inspector. It was he who approached me.' She looked more amused than annoyed. 'You see, I already have a perfectly satisfactory financial adviser, someone I trust implicitly, and I have no intention of dispensing with his services. Even if I had, Noel Murray would not be my choice of a replacement for him.'

It was an interesting development and one that Finch knew he'd have to play very carefully in order to take advantage of it.

'I see. May I ask why?'

He hoped he'd chosen the right tone of voice, intrigued but not so curious that she might regret having made the comment and withdraw it.

To his relief, he had evidently chosen correctly for she asked, head on one side, 'Have you met Noel Murray?'

'Yes; as a matter of fact, I have.'

'And what did you make of him?' When he hesitated, she resumed control of the conversation. 'How foolish of me to ask! Of course, as a police officer, you can't be expected to make comments on a potential witness; perhaps even a potential suspect.'

The last remark was followed by a fractional pause and the delicate raising of one eyebrow, but Finch's expression remained perfectly bland, giving nothing away and, rather than lose the advantage, Mrs Gunter continued as if nothing had happened to interrupt the flow.

'I'm sure you'll agree that Noel is a very charming young man; very persuasive and excellent company, but he's what my mother's generation used to refer to as a bounder. And I know what I'm talking about, Chief Inspector. I was married to one for several years. Men like Teddy, and Noel Murray, may be charming but they are also untrustworthy,

151

selfish and totally unaware of other people's needs and feelings; or, if they are aware, they dismiss them as being unimportant. I believe psychiatrists have a term for people like them.' She tilted her head in Finch's direction, inviting him to join in and supply the phrase but he refused to play her game and merely nodded to show he understood her point. She gave him a long, shrewd look before continuing.

'I recognised Noel Murray immediately. He was Teddy all over again. But it amused me to watch him at work, so to speak. So when he suggested he call yesterday afternoon to discuss my investments, I agreed. You see, there's very little excitement in the village. Everyone is so worthy and so dull. Noel Murray was quite a little divertissement, I'm glad to say. Of course, I didn't accept his offer to re-invest my money. That would have been extremely foolish. But sometimes I like playing little games myself; it passes the time very pleasantly. So I pretended I might be interested and asked him to come back the following afternoon; yesterday, in other words.'

It was an excellent moment to turn the interview his way and Finch asked with an innocent air, 'What time did he arrive, Mrs Gunter?'

'About three o'clock.'

'And when did he leave?'

152

She was too intelligent not to be aware of the significance of the question and, having regarded Finch for several seconds with her head on one side and a shrewd look in her eyes, 'A little before half past four'.

'You're sure of that?' he asked.

'Not to the exact second but I happened to look at my watch soon after he left.'

She glanced at it again, a hint perhaps that it was time he also went? Not wanting to alienate her by outstaying his welcome at this early stage of the enquiry, Finch thanked her and got to his feet. If necessary, he could interview her again another time.

She waited until he and Helen Wyatt had thanked her and said goodbye and had turned away in readiness to walk back to the house across the lawn, before adding a last comment. It was, he suspected, a deliberate piece of timing on her part.

'Oh, by the way, Chief Inspector,' she said, raising her voice a little. 'While Noel Murray was here, it occurred to me to wonder why he left London and came to Northorpe. It's hardly the ideal place to run a financial consultancy, is it? But perhaps he's a keen birdwatcher—a twitcher, I believe they're called. And speaking of names, the term I was trying to remember a little while ago is "personality disorder".'

Having made her point, which Finch suspected she had saved on purpose as a parting shot, she made clear her dismissal of him by putting on her sunglasses and picking up her book.

On the way back to the car, Finch exchanged a wry smile with Helen Wyatt.

'A feisty old lady,' he commented.

'As well as infuriating,' Helen added.

'That, too. But she could be right about Murray. It crossed my mind after we'd interviewed him to get Kyle to check him out on the NPR. Leasing that house he's living in must cost a packet and, as Mrs Gunter pointed out, it seems odd he left London for somewhere like Northorpe, where the chances of finding clients must be pretty minimal. It's certainly worth looking into. As for the timing, if he left Mrs Gunter's about half past four and drove to Chelmsford along the Foxton road, he'd almost certainly have passed Charlotte Lambert on the way. I wonder what time he arrived at Jocelyn Harvey's shop.'

'Do you want to check that out now?' Helen asked.

'No; she'll be at the shop now and I'd rather I interviewed her at home.' He glanced at his watch. 'Stapleton and his men should be working their way into the village by now. Let's see how they're getting on. If it's possible, I'd also like to take a look at those ruins while they're searching them.'

CHAPTER SIX

The search party had indeed reached the village, as they discovered when they left Mrs Gunter's house and drove off in the direction of Northorpe Hall. A lay-by on the outskirts, formed when a steep S-bend had been replaced by a straighter stretch of road, was now occupied by a mobile canteen and a caravan for use as a temporary incident room. Posters asking for information about Charlotte Lambert's disappearance and requesting volunteers to help with the search of the surrounding area were already on display, featuring the photograph of the missing girl that Sergeant Bridger had obtained and a copy of which Finch had seen the day before. As they drove past, her face with its wide-set eyes seemed to follow them with a look of mute appeal.

Seeing it, Finch was struck again by her beauty and by the thought that some of these missing-person posters aroused in him—that the individuals pictured in them were not only lost but were already dead.

As for the search itself, it had reached Northorpe Hall. The minibuses that had brought the men from Chelmsford were parked along the verge with an officer on point duty ready to direct traffic past them; not that he was needed; the road was empty.

Stapleton had evidently contacted the firm in charge of security at Northorpe Hall, for the tall, mesh gates were open and another policeman was on duty logging the names of everyone coming and going from the scene and to keep out members of the public, which so far consisted of one man with a bike who was watching from the far side of the road and who cycled off when the PC swung open the gates to allow Finch and Helen Wyatt to enter on foot.

Passing through the gates was like entering another world, composed of the leaves and branches of an overgrown shrubbery that stretched out in all directions, above them and around them, so that they seemed drowned in foliage. It gave the place a strange, green underwater gloom, as if they were treading across the bed of an ancient sea. It smelt different, too. A heavy odour of moist vegetation and damp leaf-mould filled the air. It was a secretive, silent, lost kingdom, like the forest in the fairy-tale of the Sleeping Beauty.

But when they finally emerged from the undergrowth into a relatively open area of worn gravel, they were confronted not by an enchanted castle but by the ruined walls of an eighteenth-century house, roofless and windowless, which nature was already reclaiming as its own. Ivy scrambled in and out of the window openings and self-seeded saplings grew inside the building. In some places, they had even established themselves in cracks in the walls, where they clung, sprouting out at strange angles but still alive in the desperate struggle for survival.

The front door, including its casing, had gone but the steps up to it were still there and broken stumps showed where two pillars had once stood supporting the portico. Beyond it, the rooms, distinguished by the remains of interior walls in which fireplace openings were still visible, were open to the sky and weeds grew tall in the empty spaces where the floors had once covered the foundations. Nettles and brambles seemed to like it there and also willow herb, which Finch remembered reading somewhere had sprouted in profusion on London's bombsites after the Blitz and had earned itself the name of fireweed.

It was too dangerous to attempt to cross the gutted interior of the building—God knows what hazards lay hidden beneath the leaves and wild flowers, although three of Stapleton's men, sticks in hand, had braved the dangers and were wading through the undergrowth, slashing it down as they went. Instead, Finch led the way round the building to the rear, where the grounds opened up, revealing a large expanse of rough grass, once a lawn, and its surrounding borders, which had mostly reverted to scrub and trees, although some vestiges of the original herbaceous garden clung bravely on. Here a rose bush, gone wild, sent out long thorny suckers and a few fragile flowers; there a buddleia, the parent plant no doubt of the seedling bushes clinging to the walls, flourished almost indecently. Facing the lawn was a stone-flagged terrace with the remnants of a balustrade running along its front edge and five broken steps leading down to the garden.

Finch imagined it in its heyday with wrought iron garden furniture set out on the flagstones and a housemaid in a white cap with long streamers serving tea to the ladies and gentlemen lounging at their ease and admiring the garden without having to make the effort to get up and walk about it.

Stapleton had, so to speak, set up his headquarters on this terrace and stood, hands on hips, surveying his men as they moved across the grass and into the surrounding wilderness of trees and shrubs. He looked, Finch thought, like a general on a battlefield—Wellington, perhaps, at Waterloo, watching his troops go into battle. All he needed was a cocked hat and a telescope to complete the picture.

'No luck?' Finch asked as he and Helen joined him.

'Not so far,' Stapleton replied. 'It's a hell of a job, though. The bloody place is like a jungle.'

'Ideal for hiding a body,' Finch remarked.

158

But he wasn't there to exchange chit-chat with Stapleton. 'Mind if I stroll about on my own?' he went on. 'I'd like to see the place for myself.'

'As long as you keep behind my men,' Stapleton told him. 'I don't want any one wandering about on their own until that area's been searched. Ask Sergeant Hollis over there where it's safe to go.'

'Will do,' Finch agreed and, nodding to Helen to follow, set off down the steps leading from the terrace.

He would have preferred to be alone, unaccompanied by anyone, including Helen Wyatt. Exploring the place was like a childhood adventure, which he preferred to revel in by himself. Stapleton had described it as a jungle and he was right. Making one's way through the dense undergrowth was like following in the footsteps of Dr Livingstone into unexplored territory, one man pitting himself against the perils of the unknown interior of the dark continent. Ridiculous, of course, and he smiled to himself at the absurdity of the comparison. All the same, some residue of the schoolboy thirst for adventure and danger set his pulses racing.

They came across Sergeant Hollis soon afterwards, standing at the edge of a small clearing in conversation with a group of men. At Finch's enquiry, he waved a hand towards the right.

'One of the search parties has just finished with that area. You'll see it's marked off with tapes. By the way,' he added as Finch thanked him and moved off, 'are you looking for anything in particular, sir?'

'No; just having a general nose around,' Finch replied with studied indifference. 'Getting a feel for the place.'

'If you're interested in caves, you'll find what you're looking for,' Hollis told him.

The meaning of this remark was made clear a few minutes later when, having ducked under the tape marking off this section of the garden, Finch came to an arched entrance in a rocky outcrop, half concealed under stunted bushes, which at first he had assumed was a natural feature. It was only when he got closer that he realised it was a man-made cave, or better still, a grotto; one of those garden follies which were popular with the wealthy a couple of hundred years before. Narrow blades of sunlight pierced through the canopy of leaves and gave a dramatic air to the setting, like spotlights in a theatre lighting up a woodland backdrop.

Helen had not accompanied him; she had remained behind to talk to Hollis, or rather Hollis was talking to her, and Finch was glad to be alone as he pushed open the rusting iron gate that closed off the entrance to the grotto and stepped inside.

There was something about the place that

immediately caught his imagination. It was like walking into a small underwater cavern, an illusion heightened by the diffused green light cast by the overhanging trees and the tremulous, watery reflections flickering across the ceiling and the rear wall where a rivulet of water slid down over the rocks to splash into a small pool at its foot. Its sound filled the place with a liquid, rhythmic murmur, which was peaceful and yet at the same time melancholy. The air smelt of water, too, and wet rock and leaves and damp soil; the odour of wells and old, neglected churches.

But it was the statue of the girl that made the greatest impact on him. On first entering the grotto he had, for one shocked moment, thought it was the missing girl, Charlotte Lambert, standing there in the watery half-light, holding out her arms in dumb appeal. It was only after his eyes grew accustomed to the gloom that he realised it was a figure of a water nymph, or perhaps of a young goddess of the stream, which the ancient Greeks might have set up to embody the unseen spirit of the grotto and give shape to its magical powers.

For the place was special. Running his hand over the statue's marble shoulder and feeling it cool and hard under his fingers, he was convinced now that Charlotte Lambert was dead. It was a completely intuitive response that had no rational explanation except that the place smelt and sounded of death, to which the figure of the girl seemed to give a physical existence.

Turning away, he walked out through the entrance, closing the iron gate gently behind him.

He found Helen Wyatt still in conversation with Sergeant Hollis. She had apparently already asked the question Finch himself had intended to put to the Sergeant: Were there any signs of someone breaking into the grounds?

It seemed there were and Hollis, a little self-importantly, taking on the role of showing a senior officer what was what, led the way to the far end of the garden where, standing in a clump of nettles, he pointed a dramatic finger at the security fence. Two of the metal uprights had become loose in the ground, either by accident or design, and the mesh, which had partly collapsed, had been trampled down almost to ground level.

Stepping forward, Finch took a closer look.

The nearby undergrowth showed signs of having been deliberately broken, the cleaner wood where the twigs and smaller branches had been snapped off showing up quite clearly. Some of the longer strands of bramble had also been bent back to allow a clearer path into the garden. There were no clues, however, as to who might have forced this entry, no woollen threads snagged on thorns, no torn-off coat buttons lying on the ground such as

162

Sherlock Holmes might have found had he been investigating the case. Anyone could have done it; local children, lovers looking for somewhere quiet, or curious people from the village simply wanting to explore the ruins.

It could, of course, have been Charlotte Lambert's killer breaking his way in to hide her body, but instinct told him this was unlikely now that he had seen the place for himself. Entry into the grounds was not easy and the man—and he was damned sure it was a man—almost certainly was in a car. It would therefore make much better sense for him to have driven the body some distance away and hidden it in a wood or a field that had some access from the road, a lane, for instance, or a bridlepath.

All the same, the place would have to be searched even though the odds were against her body being there.

It was a conclusion he put to Helen Wyatt as they walked back to the car, although he put it more simply.

'It's too close to the village,' was all he said.

Even so, instead of getting into the car immediately, he walked through the open security gates on to the road, where he stood for several moments looking about him. To his left, the entrance to Murray's house, The Lawns, was just visible.

To his right, Lambert's house was more easily discernible. A portion of the end gable

163

stood out quite clearly. As he looked, there was a sudden flash of light as the sun was reflected back from glass. A window in the gable had been abruptly closed. Someone— obviously Lambert; who else could it be?—had swung it shut. What intrigued Finch was the reason for Lambert's presence in what must be the attic of the house. Was he watching the police come and go as they went about their search? It seemed likely. The window would be an ideal lookout point and would give him a clear view of the road and the entrance to Northorpe Hall.

Turning away, he strolled back to the car, wondering if Lambert's interest in the search had any more significance than a father's natural concern about the investigation into his daughter's disappearance and, if his own hunch was right, and he was damn sure it was, into her murder as well.

CHAPTER SEVEN

Sunday, 20th July.

As Finch told me yesterday, the search has been extended into the village. I'd heard a lot of traffic, much more than usual, coming and going all morning and, in the end, I went up to the attic to see if I had a better view of the road from the window up there. Although the trees are partly in the way, I could see the gates of Northorpe Hall, which are now set open. The police seemed to have arrived in force. There was a line of minibuses parked along the verge with a man in uniform on point duty. They were certainly well organised and I suppose I ought to be grateful, but I can't help feeling they're wasting their time. I'm now convinced M wouldn't have hidden Charlotte's body there. It's too near his house and, assuming that's where he killed her, he'd have found it difficult to carry her body through the field at the back and into the grounds of Northorpe Hall. Charlotte is— was—quite light but dead she would be a heavy burden for anyone to carry that far. No, he would have driven her somewhere else, miles away, perhaps even into the next county.

Oddly enough, now I'm quite sure she's dead, I feel much calmer, although part of me still doesn't believe that I'll never see her again. I feel as I did when my mother left, that she's simply a long way away, leaving a huge empty void where her presence used to be.

But coming up to the attic has opened up the old wounds not only of my mother's defection but of Laura's death as well. The casket containing her ashes is where I left it in my bureau when we first moved into the house. It's often occurred to me that I ought to bury it and bring her death to a closure, as today's jargon expresses it. I had, in fact, thought of placing her ashes under one of the rose bushes in the garden Charlotte designed and holding some sort of simple ceremony for the two of us. It seemed apt; but it can, of course, no longer take place. Nor will the rose garden be planted. But I've come to one decision—to keep the casket until Charlotte's body is found—if it is ever found—and then the two of them, mother and daughter, can be buried together.

I remember someone once remarking on the apparent tendency for human beings to inherit not only physical or psychological qualities from their predecessors through their DNA but patterns of destiny as well. He was referring, I think, to the Kennedy family and its history of sudden, violent deaths. If that theory is true, then it would seem predetermined that all the women I have loved should not be given a final, known resting place. I have no idea where my mother is buried. Charlotte's body hasn't yet been found. Laura's ashes are still waiting to be interred. The only funeral I witnessed was my father's; and, of course, the disposal of M's substitute mannikin under the oak tree in Hangman's Grove all those years ago and which was, I suppose, a form of burial. I'd almost forgotten that strange rite. But, reminded of it, it came back to me in a series of vivid, flashing images of the little wax figure and the biscuit tin with the picture of the Scottie on the lid and the great roots of the tree stretching out like grasping hands.

Later this evening when the police have left and the search of Northorpe Hall is over, I intend going to the grotto and leaving some flowers in Charlotte's memory and as an offering to propitiate whatever goddess or spirit of the place resides there to atone for the desecration which Finch and his colleagues have caused by trampling over it.

CHAPTER EIGHT

Finch spent the rest of the afternoon at Divisional Headquarters, conferring with Detective Chief Superintendent Mike Sanderson on certain aspects of the case, such as the organisation of volunteers to help with a search of the fields round Northorpe and the timing of a press conference. The case had roused a great deal of interest in the newspapers, largely because of Charlotte Lambert's deafness and the fact that she was young and pretty—the perfect victim, in other words, Finch thought sourly. He left it to Sanderson to take charge of the conference. As well as being the senior officer in overall control of the case, Sanderson was better than Finch at handling the press.

Remembering Mrs Gunter's advice, he also briefed Detective Sergeant Kyle on enquiring into Murray's London background, having first let the Met know that one of his officers would be coming on to their territory and might ask for their assistance if needed.

More crucially, there were the reports from Stapleton and the detectives who had carried out the enquiries along the Foxton road, in particular those of the passengers stranded at Hoe Green when the bus had broken down. All of them stated that only two cars had passed them in the forty minutes between the breakdown, when Charlotte Lambert had set off to walk home, and the arrival of the replacement bus. The drivers of both these vehicles had been identified and interviewed.

The first was a Mr Bentham in a Ford Cortina who, with his wife, was returning to Hoe Green from Northorpe where they had been visiting their daughter. Both of the Benthams had seen a young, fair-haired girl wearing a blue and white striped dress, which Mrs Bentham had recognised as the uniform of Hillside school, walking towards them in the Northorpe direction a 'short distance from the bus stop at Hoe Green'.

The second vehicle, a Mitsubishi pick-up van, was driven by a Mr Stan Cooper, a local builder and decorator, who was returning from Foxton where he'd been painting the exterior of a bungalow, to his house on the Nettleden road on the far side of Northorpe. He'd also seen a girl answering Charlotte Lambert's description, walking towards Northorpe 'some little way down the road from Hoe Green'. In fact, it had crossed his mind to offer her a lift but had changed his mind. 'You never know what girls these days might say' was the excuse he gave for not stopping. It was an enigmatic remark that DC Pearce, who had interviewed him, interpreted as anxiety on his part that he might later be accused of rape. On reading that part of the report, Finch gave a sardonic smile. Fate, it seemed, was not on Charlotte Lambert's side that afternoon.

To sum up the evidence, three witnesses, the Benthams and Cooper, had seen a girl, almost certainly Charlotte Lambert, walking down the Foxton road at different times.

The problem was working out exactly when these two sightings had occurred. The only positive time on which they could be based was 16.32 p.m. when the bus driver had called his depot on his mobile phone to report the breakdown. As well as checking the time on his watch, it had also been logged at the office. So that timing, at least, was established. The timings of the two separate sightings, by the Benthams and Stan Cooper, therefore had to correlate with that.

However, it was not a straightforward equation. None of the three witnesses had any precise idea when they had seen the girl, which left only the distance she had walked from Hoe Green. Starting out at about 16.32, they had to work out when a fourteen-year-old, walking 'quite briskly', as Mrs Bentham had described it, was likely to have arrived at the two separate locations where the Benthams and Cooper had seen her.

It took two DCs, Hammond and Fletcher, an hour and a half to solve the equation literally on the ground with the help of the three witnesses. First, the Benthams had to be driven along the route at the speed Mr

170

Bentham said he was travelling at the time and then he had to point out the place where he had seen the girl; or, at least, as near to it as he could remember. His wife corroborated both the speed and the place. The distance between that point and Hoe Green was then measured.

Then Cooper was fetched, a little unwillingly, from the decorating job in Foxton to go through a similar test.

From these measurements, the timings were then assessed and handed to Finch, so that he could check the DCs calculations.

Finch sat over them for at least twenty minutes, pocket calculator in hand. At school he had never much cared for maths, particularly those problems that involved the use of the algebraic formula: 'Let X represent the unknown factor'; in this case, the time.

But it seemed the DCs, whether through luck or judgement, had worked out the sums correctly. At least, their answers agreed with Finch's and, more importantly, with DCI Middleton's, who'd taken, and passed, A level maths at school and whom Finch consulted just to be on the safe side.

From these equations, it seemed, therefore, that it was 16.35 when the Benthams had seen Charlotte Lambert and 16.39 when Stan Cooper had passed her on the Foxton road.

Approximately.

Middleton had stressed this aspect of the calculations several times. None of the figures

171

he'd been given were absolutes, he kept pointing out. No one knew precisely how many mph the girl was walking at, nor had the exact speed of the cars been established.

He had the same strict attitude to the use of apostrophes, Finch gathered, having overheard a homily by Middleton in the canteen on the lax use of that form of punctuation by young police constables in their official reports. Middleton blamed the schools.

But absolutely correct or not, Finch was satisfied with the results for he now had a much clearer idea of when the abduction must have taken place. It was a very narrow window of opportunity, a matter of minutes, and would surely help in identifying her abductor who was almost certainly her murderer as well.

At six o'clock, the time when he reckoned Jocelyn Harvey would have closed her shop and gone home, he set off with Helen Wyatt for Northorpe, stopping briefly on the way through Chelmsford to look at her boutique.

It was called Carousel and was situated in a side turning off Moulsham Street, in a little enclave of similar up-market businesses, including a Tapas bar, an expensive ladies hairdresser's and a shop selling Belgian chocolates.

It was closed, of course, but the window was uncovered allowing passers-by to stop and admire the display, which took the form of an apparent *tête à tête* between two elegant mannequins, one seated at an ornate wrought-iron table, which reminded him of Mrs Gunter's garden furniture, the other standing beside her, one hand on hip, staring disdainfully out through the window at any one cheeky enough to stop and peer. Glasses and a champagne bottle in a bucket were placed on the table.

It was difficult to decide whether the scene was meant to be taking place indoors or outside for, despite the suggestion of a garden setting, a huge display of flowers standing on the right on a decorative plinth, like a doric column cut off at the knees, suggested a drawing room.

As for the clothes, Finch had no means of judging their merit. They, too, seemed to exhibit contradictory features, one being very short, the other very long, but both had necklines cut perilously low, allowing more than a glimpse of two pairs of highly developed breasts, the sheen on their plastic surfaces gleaming enticingly under the spotlights.

He glanced sideways at Helen Wyatt as they stood together on the pavement in front of the window, hoping for some clue from her reaction, but her only response was 'Wow!' which wasn't much help. He wasn't sure if it was meant ironically or as a genuine expression of admiration.

Jocelyn Harvey's house shared certain qualities with the boutique. It was situated in a cul-de-sac of similar properties, all of which had some decorative feature to distinguish it from its fellows. Jocelyn Harvey's had the name 'Swallows' displayed on an oval plaque by the front door, and two ornate white urns which stood on either side of the porch, overflowing with pink geraniums, blue lobelia and that plant with silver leaves, its name still unknown to him. The urns reminded Finch of the dresses in the shop window—pretty and frothy, but a little too much of a good thing.

After the boutique, Jocelyn Harvey was something of a disappointment. She was certainly attractive, with a good figure and richly coloured auburn hair, which he doubted was genuine, but in the cruel glare of the late afternoon sun that shone directly on to the front of the house, she looked tired and washed out, the skin round her nose and chin coarse and shiny. He could only assume that her clothes—jeans and a white T-shirt—were not the usual garb she wore at the shop but were more comfortable clobber she'd changed into on returning home.

She showed them into a sitting room so full of lamps and potted plants and pieces of glass and china that it gave the impression of a gift shop rather than someone's home. The heavy scent of pot-pourri from a large bowl filled with dried flowers hung in the air and irritated

174

the mucous lining of his nose.

'You've come about darling Charlotte, I imagine,' she said, before Finch could open the proceedings. Sitting down on a pale blue suede pouffe decorated with tassels, she waved them towards a sofa plump with multicoloured cushions. 'It's so awful! To think that poor girl—'

'You know her, of course,' Finch put in, anxious to get down to business. The mean thought crossed his mind that, while Jocelyn Harvey genuinely cared about the girl, part of her was enjoying the drama and the opportunity it gave her to be the centre of attention.

'Of course I do!' Jocelyn Harvey exclaimed, as if amazed that anyone should think otherwise. 'I'm very close to her. And to her father as well. God knows how Alex is taking it. He must be utterly devastated. I've called at the house to leave flowers and I've tried ringing him several times but the phone seems to be cut off.' She gave a great sigh, which raised her breasts under the T-shirt. 'If only he would let me talk to him.'

'He may prefer to be alone,' Helen Wyatt remarked in the professionally sympathetic voice of someone used to handling grief and despair. 'For the time being at least,' she added to sweeten any implied criticism in the comment.

'I quite understand that,' Jocelyn replied

175

snappishly, looking hard in Helen Wyatt's direction. 'But it's at times like this that you need your friends.'

'Indeed,' Finch said agreeably, trying to smooth matters over, adding before Jocelyn could draw out the proceedings any further, 'We've come to ask for your help, Mrs Harvey.'

'Of course, of course! Whatever help you need, you've only to ask.'

'We're checking on the movements of one or two people who were out and about at roughly the time Charlotte Lambert disappeared, simply to eliminate them from the enquiry. I believe Mr Murray called on you yesterday afternoon.'

He had expected a dramatic response and he got it.

'Noel!' she exclaimed, her eyes widening. 'But you surely can't suspect him!'

'It's for elimination purposes only,' Helen Wyatt put in, repeating Finch's disclaimer. 'He came to your shop, didn't he?'

'Did he tell you that?'

'Yes, he did.'

'Oh well, I suppose it's all right then,' she replied, leaving Finch to wonder what she would have said if Helen Wyatt had not assured her that Murray had already admitted this fact. Lied on Murray's behalf? Or fudged some inadequate answer? Probably the last, he assumed. He had the impression that she wasn't subtle enough to make a convincing liar

176

and that, despite the tinted hair and the make-up, she was probably a generous and ingenuous woman at heart to whom truth would come more naturally than deception. All the same, he wasn't prepared to take any statement she might make on trust.

'Let me see,' she continued, sitting up very straight-backed on the suede pouffe, as if by her posture alone she could convince the Chief Inspector of her reliability as a witness. 'He arrived at about ten past five although I can't be sure of the exact time to the minute. But I know it was about then because I was thinking of making a cup of tea and I wondered if I should wait till he came.'

'So you knew he was going to call?'

Her eyes widened again.

'Oh, yes, Chief Inspector. It was all arranged over the phone.'

'When was that?' Helen Wyatt asked. She had discreetly produced a notebook and pen from her handbag and was jotting down notes in shorthand.

Jocelyn Harvey shot her an impatient glance. She obviously resented being questioned by a woman and, Finch suspected, by one as young and attractive as the Detective Sergeant who had, in addition, special authority. It was Finch she preferred talking to. He was a man and she felt more comfortable with him.

Helen Wyatt was sensitive enough to be

177

aware of the tension between them and she dutifully bowed her dark head over her notebook and tried to make herself as insignificant as possible. Jocelyn Harvey, taking it as submission, turned all her attention on Finch with a satisfied air.

'When did I arrange it?' she repeated, as if the question had come from Finch. 'It must have been yesterday morning.' She paused to think deeply before lifting her head with a positive movement. 'Yes, it definitely was yesterday morning. He said he was seeing a client in the early part of the afternoon but he'd come over to the boutique as soon as he could and we'd go out for a meal.'

So Murray hadn't told Jocelyn Harvey who his client was, which was an interesting omission. Whatever the relationship between them, it wasn't entirely frank, which suggested that Murray was a damn sight more devious than he liked to appear. Remembering Mrs Gunter's remarks about personality disorder and her hint that Finch might do well to enquire into Murray's background, he decided to test this out a little further although he doubted if Jocelyn Harvey knew the answers.

'So you know Mr Murray quite well?' he suggested artlessly.

She rose to the bait as he had suspected she would.

'Oh, yes, very well, Inspector!' she replied, her voice and face expressing so much happiness that Finch felt a surge of compassion for her at the thought of the inevitable disillusionment when Murray dumped her, as he almost certainly would. Not for the first time, he wondered at the blindness of some women who seemed incapable of seeing the predatory nature of men like Murray.

Although he had completed the essential part of the interview, establishing the time Murray arrived at the shop, he took her through the rest of her statement, which covered the remainder of the afternoon and evening, including the meal they'd had at the George at Church End and the time she and Murray had parted.

They apparently hadn't spent the night together, either at her house or at his, and she seemed sensitive on the subject because she continued with a little laugh as if to make light of the situation. 'Actually, he left about ten o'clock. He said he wanted an early night. For once,' she added coquettishly.

Or perhaps, Finch added silently to himself in a much more sardonic mood, he had a body at home that he had to dispose of.

There remained only a few more questions. Did she know of anyone in the village who had shown a particular interest in Charlotte Lambert? Any boyfriends she'd spoken of? Any families she was in the habit of visiting regularly?

179

The answers were all negative and Jocelyn Harvey's response to the last question, that Alex wasn't at all keen on Charlotte mixing with anyone in the village, confirmed Finch's impression he'd already made that Lambert's relationship with his daughter was unusually protective, if not obsessively so.

He asked his last question in a casual manner.

'What about Mr Murray? Has he ever met her?'

Her answer was immediate and positive.

'Heavens, no! I had the feeling that Alex isn't all that friendly with Noel.' She gave an arch smile, head tilted suggestively. 'A touch of jealousy perhaps?'

It was clear what she was hinting at—that Murray and Lambert were rivals for her attention and that consequently the two men couldn't possibly be friends. Having met Lambert, Finch doubted if this were true but made no effort to disabuse her, merely remarking mildly, 'I was just wondering if, as they're near neighbours, they met each other socially.'

Jocelyn shook her head.

'To my knowledge they've only ever met once at a party I gave a few weeks ago to introduce Noel to people in the village. I'm certain they haven't met since.'

So Murray hadn't told her of the occasion when he'd called at Lambert's house and had

180

met Charlotte, which again confirmed Finch's suspicion that there was no real candour between her and Murray, a point he made to Helen Wyatt when, having thanked Jocelyn Harvey for her cooperation, they took their leave.

'But even if Murray was deceiving her about having met Charlotte Lambert,' he concluded, 'it doesn't follow that she was lying to us about the time he arrived at the shop, which she claims was about ten past five.'

'Which would have given him time to meet her when she was walking home along the Foxton road after he left Mrs Gunter's,' Helen pointed out.

'I realise that,' Finch replied a little testily, not so much annoyed with her than with the circumstances which, although he'd given it a great deal of thought, he still couldn't think of a rational explanation which fitted all the evidence. 'The fact remains that not one of the passengers left stranded at Hoe Green after the bus broke down saw a car pass them either going to or coming from Northorpe, except the Benthams' and Stan Cooper's and they've been checked out. And yet, we know Charlotte Lambert was walking down that road so someone else must have driven past her and offered her a lift. And that car must have been coming from Northorpe, not Foxton, otherwise it would have been seen by the people waiting at Hoe Green. Now, Murray says he drove to Chelmsford along the Church End road. So, if he's our abductor, why the hell should he have been anywhere near the Foxton road area? As he himself said, it was quicker for him to use the Church End road when he left Mrs Gunter's because it saved driving back through the village.'

'Perhaps he had to call in at his house first.'

'What for?' Finch asked.

'It could be anything. Perhaps he wanted to phone someone. Or check his emails. Or pick up something he'd forgotten to take when he set off for Mrs Gunter's, like a chequebook or credit card.'

Finch moved his shoulders restlessly.

'It's possible,' he agreed not very enthusiastically. 'So if he went back to the house, it'd make more sense for him to take the Foxton road rather than double back on his tracks.'

'Passing Charlotte Lambert on the way,' Helen added.

'They'd be going in opposite directions,' Finch pointed out. 'He'd be driving towards Hoe Green where the bus had broken down, she'd be walking towards Northorpe. So what happens next?'

He asked the question more of himself than Helen Wyatt.

He pictured the scene as if he were standing on the grass verge watching the events unroll as they would on a screen, with Murray's Audi coming up from his left and approaching the girl who was coming in the opposite direction. In that imagined scenario, the two figures, Charlotte Lambert's and Murray's behind the wheel of the car, seemed frozen in a moment of time, immobile, set on divergent paths that were irreconcilable.

Then, unexpectedly, his imagination switched itself to Murray, as if he were observing the scene through his eyes—the country road, the deep verges, the trees casting long shadows over the tarmac and the figure of the girl, which seemed tiny, why he wasn't sure, walking steadily towards him.

And he'd stop. Of course he'd stop. Finch could almost see it happening—the car slowing down and stopping, Murray lowering the driver's window, the girl going up to the car to explain how the bus had broken down— although God alone knew how; she was deaf and presumably Murray didn't understand sign language—but however she'd managed to convey the situation, Murray understood and offered her a lift.

She gets into the car. Why not? She knows Murray, she's met him at her house in her father's presence, so she has no reason to be afraid of him. Murray makes a three-point turn in the road and drives back towards Northorpe with Charlotte Lambert sitting beside him. The time would then be about twenty to five, assuming Mrs Gunter's

183

estimation that Murray left her house at half past four was roughly accurate. Add another ten minutes, say, for Murray to drive back to The Lawns to check his emails or make a phone call or whatever it was he needed to do that had persuaded him to return to the house, plus another half a minute to get back in the car and drive along the Foxton road.

It was what happened after this that troubled the Chief Inspector. It was as if his imagination, having pictured so clearly the scene along the Foxton road, began to dim, like a mirror clouding over, and he couldn't envisage the next step in the sequence of events.

All right, he told himself. If his imagination was going to let him down, try logic.

So far he had Murray behind the wheel of his car, with Charlotte Lambert beside him in the passenger seat, driving back towards the village.

What would he do next?

Quite obviously, he wouldn't do what the girl expected: that is to drive her to Field Lodge. Instead, he'd turn into the driveway of his own house. At this, the girl would no doubt protest and he would have to try to calm her down with an explanation for his behaviour, using some form of gesturing as he wasn't trained in signing.

But what he could not control was his rising sexual excitement. Charlotte Lambert was young, pretty, vulnerable. He was sexually experienced and assured. Women usually were only too eager to accept his advances. So, he made a pass at her, possibly only an attempted kiss at that early stage. But instead of submitting, the girl panics and fights back. Suddenly the situation has passed beyond his control. Instead of a yielding, compliant fourteen-year-old, he has a struggling, screaming adolescent in the car with him, trying to fight him off.

What happened next was easy enough to imagine, if you took the simplest and most logical development. Murray himself panics and tries to restrain her, putting his hand over her mouth to stop her screams.

And logically and inevitably, he suffocates her and he is left with the body of Charlotte Lambert beside him in the car.

What does he do next?

He sits there for a time, thinking about his next move. If he is right and Murray is a sociopath, with possibly some secret in his past that drove him out of London, it won't occur to him to send for an ambulance or the police.

His first thought would be to get rid of the body. But not yet. He has an arrangement to meet Jocelyn Harvey in Chelmsford. It will look suspicious if he doesn't turn up or arrives late once Charlotte's disappearance becomes common knowledge. So, disposing of the body will have to be postponed for the time being.

185

The next step, then, is to hide it, either in the garage or in the house itself. That done, he gets back into the car and drives off to Chelmsford, taking the road through the village to Church End, the route he said he had taken. By doing that, he disassociates himself from the girl's disappearance along the Foxton road and if anyone in the village sees him driving towards Church End, it doesn't matter. It only strengthens his alibi.

And it also explained, Finch thought, the fact that none of the people waiting for the bus at Hoe Green saw his car go past them, as they would have done if he'd taken that route. After all, a large, silver-grey Audi isn't easily overlooked.

He'd have to check the timing, of course, but Finch was sure that there'd be no problem there. The times given to him by Mrs Gunter and Jocelyn Harvey were approximate enough to allow for the extra ten minutes or so to cover the time it would have taken to have picked Charlotte Lambert up, drive her back to The Lawns and murder her.

As for getting rid of the body, he could have done that much later that evening, after he left Jocelyn Harvey's house at around ten o'clock. In fact, he could have taken as long as he liked, perhaps even driving into Suffolk to dispose of it.

It all seemed to hang together perfectly reasonably and yet the scenario he'd built up in his mind didn't quite add up. The main stumbling block as far as he was concerned was the question of how he'd communicated with the girl. The image of Murray using some crude, amateur sign language seemed somehow ludicrous and illogical compared with the rest of the theory. However much he tried, he simply couldn't *picture* the situation and, for that reason, he had no absolute faith in it.

Unless, of course, the girl could lip read. He'd have to check that point with Lambert.

And thinking of Lambert, it occurred to him quite strongly that, given a choice between Murray and the girl's father, there was much to be said for Lambert as the murderer. There'd be no problem of communication: Lambert was presumably adept at using sign language. The theory would also fit in much better with the timing and the statements given by the witnesses at Hoe Green. Of course they hadn't seen Lambert's car pass them, either coming or going along the Foxton road. There would have been no need for him to travel that far along the route. When the bus failed to arrive at Northorpe at ten to five, Lambert would have realised something was wrong and, being the over-protective father he quite clearly was, it would have been perfectly natural for him to get into this car and drive part of the way along the Foxton road looking for his daughter, meeting her somewhere on the outskirts of the village. And it would also have been perfectly natural for her to accept a lift home from him when he drew up beside her.

As for Murray, he would no longer be in the frame. He would have done what he said he had and taken the Church End road out of the village when he left Mrs Gunter's.

Means and opportunity. They were staring Finch in the face. It was motive he baulked at and he realised it had bothered him from the start. It implied an incestuous relationship which, if not overt, was certainly present in Lambert's attitude to his daughter.

But hadn't he suspected something like that from the very beginning of the case, even before he had met Lambert? When he'd first seen Field Lodge, it had immediately reminded him of the fairy story of the princess in the tower, deliberately shut away from any suitors who wanted to carry her off and marry her.

Supposing Charlotte had expressed an interest in a boy, one of her fellow pupils at Hillside? Or someone in the village? Even Murray? It could have been enough to enrage Lambert, particularly in the case of Murray. It might also explain Lambert's reluctance to mention Murray during that first interview in connection with his daughter, even though he might seem the obvious candidate for her murder.

So what could have happened?

Start at the beginning, he told himself.

Lambert picks his daughter up as she walks along the Foxton road and drives her back to Field Lodge. At some point, Murray's name comes up; perhaps as they pass his house. Once home, the situation develops into a confrontation, Lambert furious because she has made it clear she's attracted to Lambert, [*Murray*] she annoyed by his over-protective attitude to her. He loses his temper, strikes her and, in the struggle that follows, kills her.

He sat up suddenly in the passenger's seat, excited by the theory that seemed to answer a lot of the drawbacks to the other scenarios, and was aware that Helen Wyatt had turned her head in his direction and was watching him with some concern.

'Are you all right?' she asked. 'Only you seem very quiet.'

'Thinking,' he replied shortly. 'Only thinking.'

He decided to say nothing to her yet about his theory. It would need a lot more thought and checking over before he brought it out into the open.

189

CHAPTER NINE

Thursday, 24th July. 3 a.m.
I waited until half past one this morning before leaving the house. It was strange to be outside again after the six days I've spent shut between these four walls, and I felt oddly exposed and vulnerable, prey to all sorts of unseen dangers, as I suppose a small creature must feel when it leaves the safety of its burrow. At the same time, I was exhilarated and all my senses seemed unusually alert, as if a membrane had been stripped away from them and I could hear and smell and taste and see and feel much more intensely than normal.

The air was warm and walking about in it was like immersing myself in clear, tepid water. The sky, too, was clear. It seemed to soar away into infinite space and, although there was no moon, the stars were huge and I could see quite easily once my eyes got used to the low light. It altered perspective, so that the trees along the edge of the road seemed immense and the road itself was a great spreading river of darkness, the depth of which I couldn't at first estimate.

I'd picked some roses from an old bush in the back garden, which I'd meant to dig out but hadn't got round to doing. The red petals seemed black in the starlight and they had a sweet, heavy fragrance, much stronger than their daytime scent. I was planning to put them in the grotto at the feet of the statue, as a kind of benediction perhaps, or an atonement for the desecration by the police—I wasn't too sure myself of my exact motives, although the gift of flowers seemed a suitable offering.

Like the perfume of the roses, noises, too, were magnified and I realised, as I hadn't done since I was a child, that the silence of the night is a misconception. There is no silence. Instead, there's a whole concerto of tiny noises: the shifting rustle of leaves, the dry scratching of invisible creatures in the dead grass in the bottom of a hedge, even the distant insect hum of traffic miles away along the by-pass.

I stood for several moments at the side of the road, listening to these night sounds, alert to any noise of an approaching car, but also to gather up my courage to wade forward into the knee-high shadows cast by the trees.

It took about twenty minutes to cross the fields and follow my usual route to the back of Northorpe Hall. I knew exactly where the fence was flattened and I was deeply perturbed when I couldn't find it. The opening had gone.

At first, I though I had misjudged its position in the semi-darkness, but I knew I hadn't. Just inside the fence, a few yards from the gap, there is a large oak tree. I could see the great, black hump of it outlined against the stars and I ran my hand along the mesh, like a blind man, feeling for the opening. It was no longer there.

And then I realised with a shock what must have happened. Someone, Finch perhaps, had reported the break in the fencing to the security firm, who'd sent some men out to mend it. Thinking back, I could work out when this must have taken place. After the police had gone, I had a shower and then went to my bedroom, which is at the back of the house, to lie down and fell asleep. It was a deep sleep, such as I haven't had since Charlotte disappeared, like descending into a dark well of oblivion. It must have been then that the security men arrived.

I stood at that fence, my fingers hooked into the mesh, and wept as I haven't done for years; not even for my mother or Laura or Charlotte. To be shut out of the garden and its grotto was another form of death. It seemed to symbolise the death of all hope and consolation, all love and forgiveness. Something broke inside me, which I know can never be repaired.

Later, when the weeping stopped, that loss was replaced by an overwhelming rage and a lust for revenge. I came to a decision that seemed to be formed inside that rage.

M has to die. There is no other alternative. Only then will closure be achieved.

CHAPTER TEN

Over the next three days nothing very much happened. It was a state of affairs that frequently occurred but one to which Finch had never become entirely reconciled. After the initial flurry of activity following Charlotte Lambert's disappearance and the immediate enquiries it gave rise to, everything seemed to go quiet. The search for her body continued, of course, spreading out over a larger and larger area of land. But nothing was found. The door-to-door enquiries were also extended to take in the whole of Northorpe and Foxton, as well as every house between Northorpe and Church End. But again, nothing of any use to the investigation was turned up, except confirmation of certain negative facts that were nevertheless important to the enquiry.

So while no one had seen Murray's Audi on the Northorpe to Foxton road or, come to that, on the Northorpe to Church End road at the time when the girl must have disappeared, proving nothing of course, there was confirmation that a man and a woman, answering Murray's and Jocelyn Harvey's descriptions, had indeed dined at the George at Church End, leaving at about nine p.m. as they themselves had stated. One of Jocelyn

Harvey's neighbours had also confirmed that a car, presumably Murray's, had driven away from Jocelyn Harvey's house not long before ten o'clock. The witness was positive about the time. He had gone upstairs for a shower and, hearing voices, he'd looked out of the window and seen a large, silver-coloured car turning out of the close.

Enquiries at Scotland Yard into Murray's past had been even less productive: they had nothing on him in their files, although Kyle, using his initiative, had looked Murray up in a London telephone directory for the previous year and had found his old address in Chelsea. He was going to make enquiries of Murray's former neighbours, which might turn up something of interest.

Apart from that one hopeful possibility, it seemed the whole case was getting bogged down in negatives.

Up to a point, Finch was sanguine about this. Many cases he'd investigated in the past had involved hours and hours of diligent enquiry which had at first produced sod all. But despite this relaxed attitude, he began to fret at the lack of progress. It was like that Greek legend about a man, whatever his name was, shoving a bloody great rock up a hill, only to have it roll down just as he reached the top. Surely someone somewhere had seen something? But, as the days went by, he was forced to admit to himself that the case was petering out.

At times like this, a sort of bloody-minded stubbornness took over. He'd damn well make sure something did happen by pulling out a few more stops. At his insistence, the television appeal was broadcast at which Detective Chief Superintendent Sanderson, who had the better profile, was the star. Nothing came of that either, although a lot of people phoned in with their own theories. Were there any gypsies in the area at the time of the girl's disappearance? Or tramps? Or escaped patients from Roxton mental hospital? Or migrant workers?

The answer to all of them was 'No', although Finch was sourly amused by the choice of social outcasts on whom the public's suspicions could be pinned. Tramps and gypsies were old bugbears; migrant workers was a new one to him.

The organisation of local people to augment the police search party also took up time. It was arranged to take place on the following weekend, when most people would be at home, and a rendezvous point was established outside the village hall where volunteers could be registered and given printed instructions on what to do and where to go. On the map, the designated area seemed a tiny proportion of the real countryside. But, as Finch told himself, it was better than nothing and it would act as a boost both to public and official morale, both of which were low.

The other activity that needed careful planning was the re-enactment of Charlotte Lambert's last walk along the Foxton road, which was arranged to take place on the Friday at exactly the same time she was last seen.

While this was being organised, Finch took the opportunity to call on Derek Bradshaw, whom he hadn't yet personally interviewed. It was Detective Sergeant Willard who had spoken to the man on the Saturday, the day after Charlotte Lambert's disappearance. According to Willard's report, Bradshaw had an alibi for the crucial time when Charlotte Lambert had last been seen. One of Bradshaw's customers, a Mr Richard Powell, had rung Bradshaw's printing firm and spoken to the man at just after twenty past four. Willard had checked this with Powell, who confirmed the statement, including the timing of the call. He had phoned from home, he stated, and, not long after he rang off, the clock in his sitting room had chimed the half hour.

So, if Bradshaw was in his shop at Dewsbury at 4.20, it followed that he couldn't have been in the Foxton road area at about the same time Charlotte Lambert disappeared. Willard, with exemplary initiative, had timed the route himself. It had taken him nearly twenty minutes to drive from Bradshaw's shop to Hoe

Green, where the bus had broken down and Charlotte Lambert had set off to walk home.

Checking the map before setting off himself to drive to Dewsbury, Finch realised that the road there was not only an extension of the main Chelmsford to Foxton route but also passed through Banfield, where Hillside, the school for the deaf that Charlotte Lambert had attended, was situated. In fact, judging by the map, the school was close to the road and it might be worth while, as he was in the area, to stop and take a look at it. There was no point, he decided, in interviewing the head mistress, a Miss Holden. DS Kyle and DC Williams had already taken a statement from her, which was largely negative: no male staff had been absent on that Friday afternoon; no pupils had been absent either; and no, Charlotte Lambert did not have any boyfriends among the pupils. Acting as *loco parentis*, Miss Holden kept a very strict eye on any relationships between her students. As for Charlotte herself, she was a popular, mature girl who would not have accepted a lift from a stranger. In fact, and it was one of the few positive pieces of information to emerge from the statement, Charlotte Lambert was an excellent swimmer and tennis player. Had someone tried to abduct her, she would have put up a struggle.

It was a minor point but one that supported Finch's gut feeling that whoever had taken

Charlotte had been someone she knew, not a stranger.

Hillside stood on a grassy slope and it was possible to get a good view of it from the roadside. A large Edwardian mansion, it was built of pale, biscuit-coloured brick with trimmings of even paler stone round the doors and windows. Newer buildings of matching brick, some of them flat-roofed and all with large windows and carefully positioned trees, clustered around it. Between these trees and buildings, he caught glimpses of tennis courts and playing fields. A broad, gravelled drive led up from the main gates, edged with borders of shrubs, while beside the entrance a large board, embellished with the school's crest and motto in gold paint, gave further details about the establishment and what it had to offer its prospective students.

Although fees were not mentioned, just by looking at the place, Finch could guess that it would probably cost quite a lot of money to send a child there. Lambert, he thought, probably could just about manage it. Field Lodge gave the impression that money was available. As for Bradshaw, remembering the shabby sitting room and the elderly car, Finch had his doubts.

Getting back into the car, he said to Helen Wyatt, 'I've seen enough. Let's move on to Derek Bradshaw's; not that he's going to be able to tell us much. He seems to have an alibi for the time Charlotte Lambert disappeared.'

In the event, Bradshaw wasn't able to tell them anything, for when they arrived at Dewsbury and parked on the forecourt of a small parade of shops where Bradshaw's premises, Print Design, was located, they found it locked and a Closed sign hanging in the glass panel of the door.

Cupping his hands, Finch peered past his reflection into the interior of the place, not that there was much to see as a large photocopier took up most of the space in the window embrasure. Beyond it, he could just make out a counter that ran along the whole of the right-hand side, with a till and various other odds and ends standing on it. Behind was a wall-hung telephone. Several display boards occupied the left-hand wall, on which were pinned samples of leaflets, posters and headed writing paper, as well a selection of different coloured papers, arranged in a fan shape. Some of these were in day-glo shades of bright pink, yellow and a particularly poisonous-looking acid green. Below these was another counter top, on which were standing a couple of pieces of equipment, photocopiers and such like, Finch assumed.

A door in the back wall, covered by a curtain, led into another room, where presumably larger printers and copiers were stored as well as supplies of paper and card. It all looked very neat and workmanlike, and very empty.

'Damn!' Finch said softly and turned away. Bradshaw's absence meant he'd have to return another day.

As he walked back across the forecourt to the car, he took a quick glance about him. Print Design was one of a small parade of other business premises consisting of a hairdresser's, a newsagent's and a dry cleaner's, converted by the look of them from a row of small Victorian houses, their front gardens asphalted over to serve as a car-park, the small-paned, downstairs casements replaced by larger windows. A notice board screwed to the end wall announced Customer Parking Only. Below it, an arrow pointed to a side opening at the end of the parade next to Bradshaw's premises, with the word Deliveries painted along its shaft, which led, he assumed, to another parking area behind the row of shops.

Dewsbury itself, or what he could see of it, was a bit of a hybrid, being neither large enough for a town nor small enough for a village, although something of the village ethos was evidently still alive and well for, as he approached his car, the door to Marilyn's, the hairdresser's next to Print Design, opened and a middle-aged woman wearing a bright pink overall and matching earrings came out on to her doorstep.

'If you're looking for Derek Bradshaw, he's

gone out,' she said.

'Have you any idea when he'll be back?' Finch asked.

She shook her head, sending the earrings swinging.

'Sorry, I can't help you,' she replied. 'I didn't see him leave. But he shouldn't be long. If he's got a lot of deliveries to make, his wife comes in on the bus to look after the shop. Can I give him a message?'

'No, don't worry. I'll call in another time,' he replied cheerfully.

He was about to turn away, when some instinct urged him to stay. He knew it was probably pointless. According to the statement Willard had taken, the owner of Marilyn's, whose name he couldn't remember, had had nothing of any use to say in the way of evidence. She'd been in the shop at the time of Charlotte Lambert's disappearance, but had been busy 'doing a perm', to quote her words, and she hadn't seen Bradshaw leave Print Design at the crucial time. So all her statement added to the evidence was a negative corroboration to Bradshaw's own account regarding the phone call he'd received. He'd been in the shop to take it; he hadn't been seen leaving the place. And that was all.

Even so, Finch couldn't leave it there. The woman, who was looking at him with an eager, almost avid expression, reminded him of Jocelyn Harvey: the same tinted hair, blonde in Marilyn's case, the same desperation to keep the years at bay, the same loneliness and longing for attention. He thought of the lines from the Beatles' song: 'All the lonely people, where do they all come from?'

Where indeed?

'It looks a decent business,' he remarked, nodding towards Print Design. 'I should imagine Mr Bradshaw's got himself a nice little earner there.'

'No, not that good, I'm afraid,' she corrected him, making a little sympathetic grimace. 'He's knows his job; I'll give him that. But I don't think the business is doing as well as he'd hoped and, on top of that, he's never really settled in down here. He's a Londoner, you see.' She managed to invest the word with a wealth of meaning—pity edged with a touch of disapproval and contempt. 'Misses the big city, I think. He often sounds off about Dewsbury—hardly any buses or shops, not even a Marks and Sparks; no cinema. Well, you can't really blame him, can you? I'd feel the same if I was in his shoes. It's not easy either, running your own business. Then there's the worry about his daughter. Some days, he looks really fed up with it all.'

'Yes, of course, I can understand that,' Finch agreed.

He was touched by her concern for Derek Bradshaw's problems when she probably had more than enough of her own. Nodding his thanks to her, he went over to the car.

'Where to now?' Helen Wyatt asked.

'We'll drop in on Lambert again,' he said, suddenly making up his mind. So far, the morning had been largely unproductive, apart from remarks made by the woman, which had revealed a little about Bradshaw's personality but hardly added any useful evidence, except merely confirming Finch's impression of the man as someone who was profoundly disenchanted with his lot in life.

But if he had hoped for something more positive from Lambert, he was disappointed. The man was almost certainly at home but wasn't answering the door. After knocking several times and receiving no reply, Finch stepped back from the porch and surveyed the front of the house. The downstairs blinds were still drawn and the windows closed, although one was open upstairs, suggesting Lambert hadn't gone out.

Taking a few paces to the right, he looked up at the attic window in the gable end and fancied he saw a movement behind the glass but it turned out to be nothing more than the reflection of branches of the nearby trees moving gently in the light breeze.

All the same, he felt the need to communicate with the man and, tearing a page out of his notebook, he wrote down a short message telling him that a reconstruction of his daughter's walk from Hoe Green along the

Foxton road would take place on the following Friday afternoon, starting at 16.32, the time when the bus had broken down, and that he, Lambert, would be very welcome to witness it if he wished to. Folding it in half, he pushed it through the letterbox and gave a final knock on the door, using the signal he and Lambert had agreed. He doubted if Lambert would turn up at the reconstruction, but he might read the note, which was at least something positive in a case which, so far, was proving to be maddeningly negative.

Clambering back into the car, he wondered dourly when the hell his luck was going to change and something, anything, would happen to get the case moving again.

CHAPTER ELEVEN

Friday, 25th July.
Finch called at the house this afternoon and left a note, telling me that they're going to stage a reconstruction of Charlotte's last walk back from Hoe Green. I shan't go to watch it, of course. It would be a torment to see someone taking Charlotte's place and pretending to be her, but I suppose the police feel a re-enactment might produce results, although I doubt it. Finch meant well, I think, in letting me know. Perhaps he is more sensitive and better at his job than I give him credit for.

I was upstairs in the attic when he came. In fact, I've been spending quite a lot of time up here. I feel safe, above it all, an observer, not a participator. As such, I've been able to watch the police come and go as they've searched the village.

They finished searching the grounds of Northorpe Hall yesterday and moved on up the road. I assume they didn't find Charlotte's body; I didn't expect them to. M wouldn't have hidden it so near to home.

There was a shower of rain last night and I lay awake, listening to it pattering against the windows as if tapping to come in, and I thought of Charlotte lying out there somewhere, her face turned up to the sky and strands of her wet hair clinging to her cheeks and forehead like the time we went walking in Suffolk along the sea wall into Southwold and got caught in that thunderstorm.

Sometimes the pain is unbearable and I feel I can't go on. I want so desperately for her to be found so that I can bury her with love and dignity. I have been thinking about this quite a lot recently and have come to a decision, which is a sort of solace. If she is found, then I'll arrange for her body to be cremated and I'll put her ashes in the urn with her mother's and bury it in the rose garden she designed so that I'll know where both of them are lying.

Please God, if there is one, let her come home to me.

CHAPTER TWELVE

As Finch had expected, Lambert was not present on the Friday afternoon at the re-enactment of his daughter's last walk home. How could he have stood by and watched as the girl, the daughter of one of the sergeants, in looks and age very similar to Charlotte and wearing the blue and white striped dress, the summer uniform of pupils from Hillside school, walked the same route along the Foxton road?

Murray failed to turn up because he had a dental appointment in Chelmsford. At least, that was the reason he gave in the telephone message he left at Divisional Headquarters for the Chief Inspector. Whether this was true or not, or whether he had chickened out, was anybody's guess.

There was, however, quite a number of people lining the route, prompted no doubt by the television appeal in which the Detective Chief Superintendent had appeared, asking for witnesses to come forward and drawing attention to the re-enactment scheduled for the Friday afternoon.

The press was also present, including TV reporters and newspaper photographers, snapping away as the girl, taking Charlotte Lambert's role, walked along the road under the trees. A small posse of police, including Finch, followed, Detective Chief Superintendent Sanderson leading the way.

The two motorists who were known to have driven along the route on that Friday afternoon also took part, but otherwise the road was temporarily closed to other traffic.

Finch took refuge behind Sanderson's broad back, making sure he averted his head whenever he spotted a photographer or a TV film crew anywhere in the vicinity. It wasn't just a dislike of having his photo taken but a feeling of the futility of it all. Of course the re-enactment had to take place. In a case involving a minor, and one who was moreover pretty as well as handicapped, it was expected that the police would go to any length to find her and punish her abductor. The likelihood of murder also crackled in the air, like the threat of a thunderstorm. It gave the occasion a buzz, like an electric charge.

Finch doubted if the same *frisson* of excitement would have been generated had the victim been a sixty-year-old housewife with swollen ankles and greying hair. He also doubted if anything of any value to the investigation would come out of the event, apart from some good PR for the police, which wouldn't come amiss, he thought wryly.

This negative mood continued later, on the drive back to Divisional Headquarters. On a sudden impulse, he signalled to Helen Wyatt to draw into a lay-by halfway along the by-pass. He couldn't face going back to the office and writing a report on the afternoon's activities. What the hell could he say? In all honesty, sod all.

What was uppermost in his mind was the image of the young girl in the blue and white striped dress walking along under the trees, moving in and out of the shadows as the sunlight fell through the leaves. She seemed to haunt his memory like a ghost and was still present as he sat there in the car, staring out through the windscreen at the stretch of anonymous concrete with its metal rubbish bin and the grass slope littered with empty crisp packets and discarded fast food containers. Even the view of the fields that stretched behind the lay-by seemed shabby and contemptible, the earth dry, ridden with thistles and docks, the distant woods nothing more than an untidy silhouette of tangled branches.

From time to time, a passing car, driving swiftly along the by-pass, disturbed the air, its slipstream sucking at their own vehicle as if it wanted to drag it along in its wake.

Finch hardly noticed. His attention was on the image of the girl in a blue and white striped dress. He wasn't even sure if it was a recollection of the living girl, Sergeant Everly's daughter, or an imaginary likeness of Charlotte Lambert. They seem to have fused in his mind into a symbol of one solitary, vulnerable schoolgirl, walking steadily in and out of the sunshine to her death.

A sudden movement by Helen Wyatt as she shifted in the seat beside him jerked him abruptly out of his brooding reverie.

'I'm sorry,' he said, clearing his throat. It seemed so long since he had last spoken that moving his lips to utter the words out loud took a huge effort. He was conscious, too, of the young sergeant's tolerance of his silence and was grateful for it. Boyce wouldn't have been so patient. He would have fidgeted about until, unable to bear it any longer, he would have burst out with some tomfool question, breaking abruptly into Finch's train of thought.

In recompense, and because he genuinely wanted to share his thoughts with her, unusual for him, who generally preferred not to expose any of his private mental world to the scrutiny of outsiders, he said, 'We're in danger of this enquiry turning out to be unsolved, if we're not careful.'

'What do you suggest we do?' Helen asked.

'Start again from the beginning,' he said, with a certainty that surprised even him. 'Go back to the original statements and re-examine them word for word. And,' he added with none of that earlier assurance, 'hope to God the re-enactment and the search over the weekend come up with something new.'

CHAPTER THIRTEEN

Wednesday, 30th July.
I didn't go to the re-enactment this afternoon. There was no way I wanted to watch someone taking Charlotte's part, repeating one of her last known actions before she disappeared.

I've seen this sort of thing on television, the rerun of events leading up to a murder, with someone who resembles the victim walking along the same route. It's usually a girl or a young woman; at least the ones I've seen have never featured a man, and the police take special care to make sure to choose someone who looks like the victim and to dress her in similar clothes. The whole thing sounds like some ghoulish carnival with TV cameras filming the whole affair.

I couldn't bear to go. There's something obscene about it, a pandering to people's voyeurism and their love of the macabre. If they brought back public hanging, there'd be no shortage of spectators. They'd flock to the event in their hundreds.

The thought has sickened me.

I've been sitting up here in the attic all day. I feel oddly more at home up here; even happy, if that's possible; certainly distanced from it all. It's like an eagle's eyrie, above the stress and despair of everyday life, looking down through the trees. No one knows I'm here, except Finch, perhaps, but he doesn't really count.

I can understand people shutting themselves away from the world and becoming recluses. The thought reminded me of the grotto, which is like a kind of hermitage. In fact, in the old days when Northorpe Hall was in its heyday, owners of houses like it would pay some elderly tenant to grow his hair and beard and sit in a cave like the grotto and act the part of a hermit to amuse the guests.

Like the hermit, I've turned this space under the sloping eaves of the roof into my own domain. I've brought a chair up here and books and the CD player, which I run off an extension cable plugged into a socket on the landing and listen to Bach and Vivaldi. I can also boil an electric kettle and make myself coffee. It's like a den, snug and closed in and, apart from the one window in the gable, has no connection with the outside world. The only intrusion I had today was the sound of voices as people from the village walked past the house on their way to watch the re-enactment. They're ghouls and I hate and despise them all.

But it's possible some good may come out of it. It may trigger a memory in one of those people who'll pass the information on to Finch. It could be something quite small, like catching a glimpse of M's Audi turning out of his drive or perhaps simply hearing the sound of its engine as it drove off along the Foxton road. It could be enough to alert Finch to M's guilt and lead to his arrest and the discovery of Charlotte's body.

I haven't prayed for years, not since my childhood in Kedstone, my father's old parish in Warwickshire, when I used to go to Sunday school in the church hall and Mrs Grant led us in reciting the Lord's Prayer. We stood, palms and fingertips pressed together as she instructed us, intoning the words 'Our Father, whichart in Heaven.' I never understood the meaning of 'whichart', associating it with witches and the black arts.

But I pray now for M's arrest. My only regret is that hanging has been abolished and he'll escape with his life. Not like Charlotte.

CHAPTER FOURTEEN

More people turned up for the mass search of the fields and woods round the village than for the re-enactment, probably because it was the weekend, the weather was good and it was something to do that was different, although Finch liked to think that some of them at least were encouraged to join in by more altruistic motives.

They arrived in their dozens, in cars, on bicycles, on foot, bringing with them, as advised, walking sticks and haversacks containing bottled water and sandwiches, although a refreshment van, selling hot drinks and beef burgers had set up in business in the car-park of the village hall. It did a roaring trade, as did the Feathers.

The result, as Finch had gloomily predicted, was a total failure. Over the two days of that weekend nothing of any use was found; not Charlotte's body, nor even a piece of her clothing. There was, of course, plenty of other people's apparel found, shoes in particular, but also pullovers, scarves, socks, even a shirt, and Finch wondered, as he had before, how it was possible in the middle of an apparently underpopulated area of countryside, for so many people to mislay so many garments.

While waiting for the results of both the re-enactment and the search, he settled down to make good the undertaking he had made to Helen Wyatt, but more particularly to himself, to start again at the beginning and go through all the reports on the case so far, although his heart sank at the prospect. He had already read through the damned things several times, from Stapleton's meticulous but fundamentally boring account of the searches he and his men had made in the area to the shorter statements collected during the door-to-door enquiries, which had taken place in all the locations that had any connection with the case from Northorpe itself to the houses along the Foxton road.

He began with the reports on the Foxton road, largely because they were in that chronological order but because logically they ought to be the most important. After all, they were taken from potential witnesses to Charlotte Lambert's abduction. The people involved bloody well lived alongside the road where the girl had disappeared. But, as he recalled them, they were all negative.

The pair of houses they occupied were called, for some unfathomable reason, Prospect Cottages, although there was no prospect visible from either of them that was worthy of comment, only flat pasture, relieved here and there by an occasional tree. The houses themselves were the architectural equivalent of their settings. Built of dull red

215

brick and slate, they sat too close to the road and had that mean look of tied cottages in which the barest minimum is considered good enough for farm labourers. The windows were too small, the doorways too narrow, the porches constructed from just enough bricks and timber to make the building of them viable. And the people who lived in them had seen and heard nothing.

With a sinking heart, Finch pulled the folder towards him and, as if paying penance, opened it and bowed his head over the badly typed pages it contained.

CHAPTER FIFTEEN

Friday, 1st August.
I awoke this morning in a new and unexpected frame of mind, which I can't account for. As far as I can remember, I had no dreams last night, which might have triggered this change of feeling; no new emotional traumas apart from the usual agony of loss and emptiness that I wake to every morning. Today was different. The pain was still there; that hadn't gone away. But something new had taken over—a sort of resolve; not the hot anger I had felt before but a cold, clear-headed determination as hard as steel. It was directed, of course, at M. But not just at him, or the police, although I feel enraged that they apparently still haven't found the evidence to arrest him. No, my fury was turned not on them so much as on myself. I am tired, tired, tired of my own lack of action; of sitting up here in this attic brooding and nursing my sorrow, constantly going over the past, remembering the old happiness, agonising over my loss. Like a rotting corpse, I am putrid with self-pity. I stink of it. I loathe myself for letting Charlotte down and putting myself, not her, first.

That is now going to change. I have promised her I will find her body. I will not allow her to be huddled away in some unknown grave, like my mother. She shall have all the rites and ceremonies due to her. But, in order for that to happen, M must be forced to tell me where she is.

When I came to that decision, I felt as if a great warm sensation flooded through me, the same as I had experienced when Charlotte was a new-born baby and I held her in my arms for the first time and felt the warmth of her tiny limbs through her shawl. That was love. This feeling is love as well, but also an overwhelming sense of achievement and well-being now that the waiting and uncertainty are over and I know exactly what I must do.

At first, it was strange going out of the house in daylight and getting into the car. I hadn't done that for days and I'd forgotten how large the sky is and how bright and far away. It was also frightening and I felt my hands shaking as I opened the garage doors and started up the engine.

I'd thought very carefully over what I was going to do, even down to the route I'd take out of the village. Obviously, I didn't want to go via Hoe Green, which would take me along the road that Charlotte had walked on her last day alive. It would also pass M's house and I'm not ready for him yet. Neither was I keen on driving through the village, where I might be seen by people who know me.

Instead, I had looked at a large-scale map of

the area and found a rarely used minor B road, which is little more than a hard-surfaced lane. In fact, studying the map, I realised that there are quite a lot of these narrow by-roads that criss-cross the countryside like tiny veins and probably started off life as green tracks in Saxon times, used by drovers and pedlars and travellers on foot.

The lane I found leads off the main Northorpe to Foxton road on the outskirts of the village and meanders through the fields and small hamlets for several miles, past farms and cottages and the occasional pub. After about ten miles, you come to a T-junction, the turning to the right taking you eventually to the by-pass and the main route into Chelmsford. After a lot of twisting this way and that, it leads on to the A12, the road into Colchester, and is the one I followed.

I went prepared. From the back of my wardrobe, I dug out an old plaid shirt I hadn't worn for years and a pair of corduroy trousers. I also made sure I had enough cash on me, so that I needn't write a cheque or use my credit card and there wouldn't be any signatures to trace back to me.

Although I know Colchester fairly well, I don't go there all that often, preferring Chelmsford or London if I have to buy anything I can't get locally. That was another reason why I chose the place: it was unlikely I'd run into someone I knew there. But to be

219

on the safe side I parked down a side street and walked into the town centre, stopping on the way to buy a baseball cap at one of those cheap men's clothing stores which sell low-price T-shirts and jeans.

Later on I caught a glimpse of myself reflected in a shop window and thought how different I looked wearing that ridiculous cap. It was pity though about the beard. It's too distinguishing a feature but I couldn't shave it off. That would draw even more attention to myself in Northorpe, and that's the place that really matters.

Buying the rest of the stuff was as easy as buying the cap. A do-it-yourself shop supplied most of it—the length of cord and chain as well as the hasp and padlock and a pair of wire cutters. I also bought some screws and paintbrushes, which I didn't really need but I thought, if questions were asked, I'd be less easy to trace if I added these other items to my list.

Carrying them out of the shop in a plastic bag, I was suddenly reminded of that time years ago when I'd collected up the objects I'd need, like the candle-ends and the old trowel, for my black magic ceremony in the woods at home. There was the same feeling of deep satisfaction in having planned the event down to the last detail.

I left the gun until last. It was the most important prop and the one that caused me the most anxiety. Finally, having walked round several shops selling toys, I found what I was looking for in a small shop specialising in puppets and models, that sort of thing. It was a handgun, its design obviously based on a genuine firearm and, considering it was a toy, was surprisingly expensive. Even so, it had a plastic sheen about it that I thought I could tone down with some black paint. So I bought a small tin of black enamel and a model-making kit for building a stealth bomber. Like the screws and the paintbrushes, I thought the paint and the kit would help cover up my tracks. In the same shop, I also found a pair of realistic handcuffs which actually locked, but which could be released with a sharp tug.

I then moved on to one of those large, anonymous supermarkets where I stocked up with fresh food, such as milk, meat, vegetables and fruit. I'd run out of supplies of these and was relying on what was left in the deep-freeze.

Once home, I roughed up the plastic on the gun a little by rubbing it with sandpaper before dabbing on little smears of the black paint to make it look less new and shiny.

It was dry by the time I left for M's house, which was about nine o'clock that evening when it was dark enough to hide my movements but not so late to make him suspicious of my calling on him. The only matter for concern was the uncertainty of not knowing whether or not he'd be alone. It would ruin all my plans if Jocelyn was there. But there was no sign of her car in the drive when I arrived.

I went by the back way across the fields, making first for the grounds of Northorpe Hall, where I stopped briefly to cut through the new length of security fence with the cutters I'd bought, trampling it down to the ground before flinging the cutters away into the undergrowth. The gun and the other bits and pieces I'd bought were in my pockets. Once the fence was down and the gap re-installed, I then moved on towards The Lawns, careful this time to approach it by the front door.

M was surprised and delighted to see me, turning on the old charm as soon as he saw who it was standing on his doorstep.

'Alex, what a delightful surprise!' he exclaimed. 'Come in, come in!'

He led the way into that dreadful drawing room of his with the pink brocade curtains and the gilt-framed mirrors, waving me towards one of the leather-covered sofas.

The man is a consummate actor. There was no sign of guilt in his face, just the initial pleasure at my arrival turning to a more suitable expression of sympathetic concern as soon as I sat down.

'My dear fellow, what can I say? I was shattered to hear about your daughter. I tried to ring you as soon as I heard but your phone seemed to be disconnected. Is there any news yet?'

'About her body being found?' I asked.

He seemed taken aback by my frankness, as if I'd broken some code of behaviour expected of a grieving father.

'No, not yet,' I replied.

'Is there anything I can do?' he asked, eyebrows raised, head tilted to one side, hands open and lying palms upwards, as if inviting me to put whatever need I had into his safe keeping.

'Yes, there is, as it happens,' I said, making my voice and manner as matter of fact as I could, although inside I was seething with rage and hate, which I found difficult to control. So as not to betray my feelings, I thrust my own hands into my pockets and clenched them hard over the gun and the other items I had brought with me. 'I want you to tell me what you've done with Charlotte's body.'

I had intended him to be shocked by the abruptness and unexpectedness of my remark, which I made in a deliberately casual, conversational manner. I wasn't disappointed. Clever though he is, M couldn't hide the effect it had on him. In a way, it was almost comic, a stage version of shock-horror even down to the physical recoil, as if to avoid an actual blow, and the dropping open of his mouth, so suddenly and completely that the tendons

223

seemed to have been severed. His eyes, however, remained wide open and motionless, fixed on my face.

There was a long moment of silence and then he began to recover. He blinked several times and, under the flesh of his cheeks, I could see the muscles scrambling to regain control of his mouth.

To give him his due, he wasn't without a certain courage. A man less in control of himself might have broken into a torrent of denial and self-defence. Instead, he replied in a calm, even voice, 'This is ridiculous, Alex. I haven't seen your daughter for weeks. What makes you think I might have killed her?'

'I don't *think*,' I replied. 'I *know*.'

'In God's name, what gave you that idea?'

'I saw it in your face.'

'When?'

'The day you called at my house to return the Northorpe Hall file. You lusted after her.'

I could see the accusation had struck home. He started to his feet and took several steps away from me towards the fireplace where he stood, his back towards me, shoulders bowed, one hand up to his forehead as if deep in thought. Then he swung round towards me. His face looked suddenly gaunt, the flesh pared down to the bone, and I thought that was how he'd look when he was old and all his physical appeal had wasted away.

He ran his tongue over his lips and when he

spoke his voice sounded dry and cracked.

'Have you said anything about this to the police?'

I held his gaze.

'No, not yet.'

'But you intend to?'

'It depends.'

'On what?'

'On whether or not you tell me where you've hidden my daughter's body.'

For a second he remained quite expressionless and then, visibly shaken, he burst out, 'I don't know! I didn't kill her!'

I got slowly to my feet and walked across to the patio doors which led into the back garden. They were open, I realised, when I drew back the curtains. M remained where he was, standing in front of the fireplace, watching me, the back of his head reflected in the mirror over the mantelpiece. I could see he was frightened and wary of what I might do next and, so as not to alarm him, I made my movements slow and controlled. With my right hand in the pocket of my jacket, resting on the gun, I took a few steps towards him, my eyes fixed on his.

'Oh, for Christ's sake, Alex, this is ludicrous. I haven't—' he began.

Before he could finish, I produced the gun, holding it so that it was partly hidden in my hand.

'Turn round,' I said.

Before he did so, he tried again to speak, his head half-turned in my direction.

'Listen, Alex—'

'Shut up!' I told him and jabbed the barrel of the gun into the small of his back.

I took the handcuffs out of the other pocket and, pulling his hands behind his back, slipped them over his wrists. Had he known, he could have broken them open with one quick jerk, but he seemed too intimidated to move. I learned then, with a *frisson* of excitement and shamed exultation, the power of the gun, and experienced what I had only partly acknowledged before: the intoxication of having complete control over another human being.

As if completely cowed, he offered no further protest and stood quite still as I took out the length of cord and fastened one end to the handcuffs so that it formed a leash about a yard long.

Once that was done, I gave it a tug and said, 'Right! Now start to walk slowly towards the patio doors. And don't speak.'

He obeyed, turning away from the fireplace, his face appearing briefly in the mirror above it. It was as closed and as tight as a fist, the bones protruding like knuckles under the stretched skin.

The garden was full of shifting light and shadows gliding across the lawn and the dark surface of the pool, quite still now that the fountain was turned off. Reflections of branches and patches of sky with moving clouds shimmered across it like a watery mirage. Its beauty almost moved me to tears, not just for Charlotte's sake and the inexpressible magic of the night but also for M himself, although I couldn't understand why. So I quickened my pace, urging him on more harshly so that, by the time we reached the boundary fence, I was infuriated by his clumsy attempt to duck under the top bar.

'Move!' I ordered him and, once he'd dropped down on the other side, he set off at a shambling trot along the edge of the field.

Getting through the hedge at the back of Northorpe Hall was easier as I'd flattened down the mesh fence to ground level, but the earth was still rough and, after he'd stumbled a couple of times, I thought it safer to slow down the pace in case he fell and broke an ankle, which would make the whole enterprise even more difficult.

As we slowed down, my own heart rate dropped and, without the sound of blood pumping in my ears and the drum beat in my chest, I was aware of other night noises, some gentle like the stirring of leaves, some, like his harsh gasping breaths, too loud and persistent.

He kept turning his head to and fro as well and I wondered why, until I realised that, despite his professed interest in the place, he had apparently never been there and was looking about him to get his bearings. This realisation made me urge him on. The sooner I got him under lock and key the better.

Once inside the grotto, I pushed him down on one of the stone benches so that his back was towards me. There was just enough light to see the statue, white and glimmering in the shadows like a ghost, and to glimpse the reflections glancing off the little waterfall. The place was loud with its liquid pattering and it suddenly occurred to me that, if I were M, I'd be driven mad by it. The thought surprised me. I hadn't imagined I would feel any pity for the man at all.

I was suddenly desperate to get out of the place. Backing away to the door, I took the chain together with the padlock and key out of my pocket and slammed the grille shut, winding the chain through the bars and fastening the padlock through two of the links, which I also snapped shut.

The noise startled M. He had got to his feet, his back still towards me, as if frightened to turn and face me.

'What's going on?' he called out. 'In God's name, Alex, what are you playing at?'

'If you pull hard on the handcuffs, you'll break them open,' I told him. 'They're only plastic. But I shouldn't bother calling for help,' I added. 'No one will hear you and the police have already searched the place, so they won't be back.'

As I turned to leave, he came scurrying awkwardly towards the gate, twisting his arms frantically to break open the handcuffs.

'Don't go!' he shouted. 'Listen! For Christ's sake, listen! Alex, I didn't kill her. I swear to God I never even touched her!'

I walked away without replying. He no longer meant anything to me at all. I felt nothing for him; no hate, no bitterness; I was empty of all feeling, even compassion and the need for revenge. His voice crying out behind me had no more meaning for me than the barking of a dog. Gradually the sound faded until, by the time I'd reached the boundary fence at the edge of the garden, I could no longer hear it at all.

CHAPTER SIXTEEN

Finch was about halfway through the pile of reports when Detective Sergeant Kyle knocked on the door and, sticking his head round it, announced, 'I've got that report on Murray, sir. Shall I give you a run-down on it now, or shall I come back later, after I've typed it up?'

'Let's hear it now,' Finch replied, secretly relieved for the excuse to take a break, adding as a sop to his conscience, 'Just the gist of it for the moment though. I've got all this lot left to read through. But come in and sit down.'

'Right!' said Kyle, drawing out a chair and settling into it. He looked pleased with himself as well he might. His enquiries in London had been successful.

'Well, about Murray,' he began. 'I talked to half a dozen people who'd known him in London; the neighbours at the block of flats in Chelsea where he'd lived had liked him, especially the ladies. It was his business acquaintances who weren't so keen. I gathered he was good at his job but a damned sight too ruthless for most of them. One of the blokes I spoke to had lost a valuable client to Murray and wasn't best pleased.

'It seemed Murray specialised in elderly women, widows mostly, who were well-off and lonely. Murray chatted them up and then raked in their business. There was one in particular, an 82-year-old widow, lived alone in a mansion flat stuffed full of antiques, no close family but plenty of money and some nice bits of jewellery as well. Evidently Murray called on her regularly to chat to her about her investments, bearing gifts, as they say, roses usually, and the occasional bottle of bubbly.

'You can probably guess the ending. Old lady dies and, lo and behold, when the Will's read, Murray's the main beneficiary. He got the mansion flat and its contents plus a fair old slice of her capital. The rest was left to various charities and her cleaning lady. Her one and only relative, a niece by marriage, lived in New Zealand and by the time she heard about the old lady's death and the Will and got on a plane for Heathrow, it was too late. The flat was on the market, the furniture had been sold and the money was in Murray's bank account. Some of the jewellery was also missing.

'I gather the police made enquiries but there was nothing they could do. It was all kosher, including the old lady's death; result of a stroke, apparently. As for the Will, that was also above-board, according to her solicitor. She had all her marbles and, in fact, remarked to her solicitor that she looked on Murray as her son. So the niece went back to New Zealand empty-handed. Incidentally, she'd never kept in touch with the aunt, not even a Christmas card, let alone roses and champagne.

'Even so, there was gossip and several of Murray's clients took their business elsewhere. But financially he was all right, of course. A couple of the people I spoke to reckoned he must have made at least two and a half million out of the estate. Anyway, as soon as the flat was sold, he cleared out of London without leaving a forwarding address; probably decided to lie low until the gossip died down.'

'What about the jewellery?' Finch put in.

'Who knows? Murray might have taken it. Or the old lady could have sold it or given it away. Or the cleaning lady could have helped herself. Anyway, there wasn't enough evidence to show what had happened to it so there was nothing the police could do. I'll put all that in my report, by the way,' Kyle continued. 'Do you want me to call on Murray?'

'I don't think so,' Finch replied. 'At least not yet. There's the Lambert enquiry hanging over him and I'd rather wait till that's sorted before we make any other moves.'

'Right!' Kyle agreed and left the room.

The information about Murray hadn't come as any great surprise to Finch after Mrs Gunter's remarks about the man, which had confirmed his own conclusions about him. All the same, it was a distraction and it was with even less enthusiasm that Finch turned to the remaining reports, all of which contained, as he had expected, nothing of any value to the

232

case.

Two hours later, he picked up the last one in the pile, not expecting any useful results from that either. It covered the enquiries made at Pelham Farm which, if he remembered rightly, was too far away for its inhabitants, a Mrs and Mrs Conway and their farm worker, Mr Jessop, who lived at number one Prospect Cottages, to have seen or heard anything that happened that Friday afternoon on the Foxton road.

And he was right. PC Williams, a reliable but unimaginative officer, had typed out their statements in an amateurish manner, summing it up in the last sentence that said what Finch himself had already concluded.

Mr and Mrs Conway and Mr Jessop had heard and seen nothing. While Mr Conway, with the assistance of Mr Jessop, was tending to some pigs in a paddock on the far side of the farmyard, Mrs Conway, who was weeding the front garden for part of the time and might have been in a position to witness something, stated at about four o'clock, she'd gone into the house to make tea. She added that it was very unusual for any cars to pass the house.

Finch, who was about to shut the folder and return it to the pile, stopped suddenly and read the last part of the report again.

The first time he had read it, he had assumed that the woman was referring to the Foxton road on which traffic was known to be

233

light. But it now occurred to him that this couldn't have been her meaning. If she couldn't see the Foxton road from the farmhouse, a fact that Williams had stated in the opening sentence of his report, then it followed that she wouldn't have been able to see it from the front garden either.

Scrabbling with the page, he turned it over to the opening paragraph and, to make quite sure, read it out loud slowly so that he shouldn't misinterpret it.

'Pelham farm,' he read, '*is situated on the right about 300 yards along Pelham lane, a turning off the Foxton road. Because of the distance and the slope of the land, as well as the trees and bushes, it is not possible to see the Foxton road itself either from the house or the farmyard, or any vehecles,* (spelt incorrectly, Finch noted) *moving along the road.*'

That was clear enough. And yet Mrs Conway had spoken of the lack of traffic going past the house. If she couldn't see the Foxton road, then she had to be referring to the lane that did run past the house.

Finch tried to picture it as he had seen it that first day when he had driven along the Foxton road, when Stapleton and his men were searching the immediate area on that Friday afternoon, but he could recall very little about it except that it was a typical narrow, country lane. Though hard-surfaced, it was worn into ruts in places and clumps of grass

234

were growing through the gravel, suggesting it wasn't used very often.

Squeezing his eyes shut, he forced himself to conjure up a mental image of it. There had been a sign low down on the left that read Pelham Lane, and a green-painted fingerpost beside it pointing up the lane, on the arm of which were the words Pelham Farm.

Like a fool, he had misread the signs, he realised; not the actual sign-posts themselves, but the other indications, its narrowness, its worn surface, its air of disuse, thinking that it served as an access route only to the farm and to nowhere else.

He glanced at his watch. It was now a quarter to eleven. Stapleton and Williams would have gone home hours ago, but he doubted if either of them would have the information he was looking for. What he needed was a large-scale map of the area, an inch to a mile, and, better still, perhaps, a visit to the place himself in daylight.

But, above all, he needed time to think through the implications of what he had discovered and time also to discuss them fully with Helen Wyatt.

*　　　*　　　*

The following morning, having found the map he needed, he quickly checked the relevant area and found that his supposition was right:

Pelham Lane was not a dead-end as he'd originally thought but a proper route, narrow though it was, which led to a T-junction. Here it divided, the right-hand branch leading to the village of Pelham. He'd seen enough. Folding up the map and shoving it into his jacket pocket, he went off in search of Helen Wyatt. Minutes later, they were in the car heading for Northorpe along the Church End route, which took them past Lambert's house.

It had been the Chief Inspector's intention to call briefly at Field Lodge, not of course to tell Lambert of the new turn the enquiry was taking—it was much too early for that—but simply to reassure the man that, despite the lack of success with the searches in the area, the investigation was proceeding and that he hoped to have good news for him before too long.

But as the car drew near to Field Lodge, he lost his resolve and told Helen to drive on.

It would be far better, he told himself, to wait until the present enquiries were completed, when he might have something positive to offer the man.

As they passed the gate, he glanced to the right. The house looked more than ever like Rapunzel's tower; isolated, withdrawn, with just the peak of its gable visible above the surrounding trees.

The Lawns looked as deserted as Field Lodge. There was no sign of Murray, no car outside on the gravel forecourt, although the man was probably at home. An upstairs window was open and caught the sun as they drove past.

Three minutes later and they were at the opening to Pelham Lane. It was a narrow entrance and Helen had to change down to second gear to take the turning. High hedges, which scraped the side of the car as they drove past, closed in the lane on both sides but, after about twenty yards, the land lifted and they topped a steep little hill which, after a short distance, dropped away and the view opened up allowing them glimpses of the countryside over hedges and through gate openings. Some of it was pasture but most was wheatfields, well-tended by the look of them. There was an air of abundance about the place in the lushness of the young corn and the thick foliage of the trees and hedges.

It was an impression borne out by the farmhouse itself. A white plastered building, it stood back from the road with a large garden in the front of lawn and flowerbeds, as carefully tended as the fields. Seeing them, Finch marvelled yet again at the capacity of some people, living miles from anywhere and with no near neighbours, to maintain their gardens with such loving care purely out of love for them, not to impress anyone else.

A little distance from the farmhouse, he told Helen to stop and, getting out of the car, he crossed the road to look back towards Northorpe before, satisfied, he got back inside. He was right. Nothing could be seen of the Foxton road, not even a telegraph pole to mark its position. In her statement, therefore, Mrs Conway must have been referring to the lane going past her house. So somewhere along its route, the lane joined up with that other road, which he had already seen marked on the large-scale map he had studied that morning.

It was another half a mile before they came to the T-junction and a sign-post standing partly obscured by the long grass of the verge. The arm pointing to the left announced Stoneleigh, that to the right, Pelham.

Even though he'd seen it marked on the map, it wasn't quite what Finch had expected, although the name made sense. Pelham Lane, Pelham Farm. There had to be a Pelham village somewhere in the vicinity.

'Right!' he told Helen, and the car carefully negotiated the tight little turn towards the village.

It wasn't much of a place—a few houses, a shop, a village hall painted white and built of wood with a verandah running the length of its frontage. It looked like a cricket pavilion, which was probably one of its functions, for it faced an open green with a pitch in the centre, sight screens at each end and a score-board to the left.

238

Next door to it was the other essential constituent of any village: the local pub; the Lord Nelson on this particular occasion, a curious choice of name for the place was miles from the sea and had no obvious connection with the navy. A sign bearing a rough likeness of the admiral swung above the entrance, at least the eye-patch and the empty sleeve, as well as the telescope thrust under the other arm, suggested the man in question even if the features looked too red and buccolic and might have better represented Farmer Giles.

But it wasn't the inn sign that caught Finch's attention. It was something in the bar window which caused him suddenly to call out, 'Stop!'

Helen Wyatt braked and swung the car on to the forecourt in a spurt of gravel where, without a word, the Chief Inspector leapt out and set off at a brisk trot for the entrance to the pub, leaving her wondering what the sudden excitement was all about.

The place had evidently only just opened for business, for the landlord was leisurely unrolling a towelling runner along the length of the counter to protect its surface from wet glasses. Apart from him, the bar was empty, quiet and tidy, ashtrays placed neatly on tables, chairs and stools arranged just so. Sunlight falling through the windows glittered on rows of glasses and bottles behind the counter and on the brass fittings of the beer handles, giving the bar a festive air.

239

A nice pub, Finch thought and, for a moment regretted Boyce's retirement. It was the sort of place he would have appreciated. The two of them could have met there for an off-duty pint and a game of darts or bar skittles.

But he had other things on his mind as he approached the counter.

Outside, Helen Wyatt sat in the car, trying to guess what had caused the Chief Inspector to go rushing off like that although, whatever it was, it didn't take him long to sort out for, within a few minutes, he came out looking jubilant.

'Well?' she asked as he climbed back into the car.

'We've hit the jackpot!' he announced and proceeded to give her a brisk account of what had happened as, following his directions, she turned on the ignition and set off along the road to the left.

CHAPTER SEVENTEEN

At six o'clock that same morning, Alex Lambert began to carry out his plan, which he had decided on during the long sleepless night. He felt curiously light, physically as well as mentally, as if he had been emptied of all the rage and despair, the longing for revenge and all human desires.

There was very little to do except to go to his bedroom, retrieve the casket from where he had hidden it in his bureau drawer, carry it out to the garden and dig a hole for it where he and Charlotte had marked out the rosebeds. Placing the urn inside it, he stood for a moment or two in silence, looking down at it before, picking up the spade, he began to shovel the earth over it.

In an ideal world, he would have planted a rose bush over it as he had first intended; a scented one, Fragrant Cloud or Ophelia, although he would have left the choice to Charlotte. Now the grass would cover it and no one would know it was there. Perhaps it was, after all, an apt ending; the final closure: anonymity.

Going back to the house, he gathered up the cardboard folder that held the pages of his journal and stood holding it in his hand, undecided what to do with it. It had been his original intention to burn it, as his father had set fire to the letters and photographs in the kitchen garden of the Warwickshire rectory. After all, fire cleanses and purifies.

Or he could bury it under the apple tree behind the garage, as he had buried the remnants of his ritual murder of M all those years before under the oak tree in Hangman's Grove.

In the end, he did neither. He simply closed the folder before carrying it upstairs to the attic, his eyrie, his place of refuge. He himself wasn't sure why and, in a vague way, it troubled him. Perhaps he hesitated to destroy it because it was a kind of document and, as such, had an intrinsic value, which mere objects did not possess. Those could be replaced; the written word, once lost, was gone for good. Like the photographs, their ephemeral nature made them precious and irreplaceable.

He placed the folder at the back of a cupboard behind a pile of children's books that had once belonged to Charlotte and, having done that, he took a last look round and then, carefully closing the door behind him, went downstairs.

It was almost finished. There was very little else to do except to find the car keys and check his wallet to make sure he had enough money to pay for petrol on the way. The other things he'd need were already in the boot of the car.

He'd seen to that soon after he'd got up.

He had twenty-two pounds and some small change, more than enough. Putting the wallet back in his jacket pocket, he let himself out of the house.

CHAPTER EIGHTEEN

The shop was open this time. As soon as Helen Wyatt parked the car on the forecourt, Finch could see the little sign hanging in the glass panel of the door that said as much. A bell above it rang shrilly as they entered.

Finch had a few seconds to look round the outer office to confirm that he had not been wrong in remembering the samples of coloured paper arranged in a fan shape on a display board on the left-hand wall and that a particular shade of day-glo yellow was among them before Derek Bradshaw emerged from behind the curtain that separated the back room from the front office.

The sight of Finch and Helen Wyatt, accompanied by two uniformed officers who waited discreetly just inside the door, must have warned him of what was to come but he remained curiously impassive, just standing there, hands dangling, wearing the same morose expression Finch remembered staring down at him through the open driver's window of their car, the only time he had had any contact with the man.

He said nothing and it was Finch who spoke.

'Derek Bradshaw, I am arresting you for the murder of Charlotte Lambert. You do not have to say anything but it may harm your defence if you do not mention when questioned something which you later rely on in court. Anything you do say may be given in evidence.'

The man listened in silence, more interested, it seemed, in his feet, which he studied with intense concentration but, to Finch's enormous relief, he went quite docilely when the two officers took him outside, where he was placed in the back seat of one of the official police cars. The other officers, who had been guarding the back door of the premises in case Bradshaw tried to make a run for it, got into the second vehicle, and then the two cars drove off.

The presence of the police cars and the uniformed men had attracted the attention of passers-by and the owners of the other shops in the little parade. Several of them had come out on their doorsteps to see what was going on, including the haggard-looking blonde from Marilyn's. Seeing them, Finch turned the hanging sign in the glass panel in the door to CLOSED and, as a further deterrent, drew down the blind. The view through the one window was already adequately blocked by the photocopier, which occupied most of the embrasure.

The half-gloom that resulted reminded Finch of Lambert's sitting room and he made a mental note to call on the man as soon as he could. In the meantime, there was nothing much he could do while he waited for the SOCO team to unload their equipment, but to saunter about, hands deliberately in pockets so that he'd not be tempted to touch anything. There was enough lying about in the way of evidence without having to search for it, including a couple of spare copies of the poster, printed on the bright yellow paper that had caught his attention in the window of the Lord Nelson, advertising a Grand Quiz Night to be held at the pub later in the month, together with extra copies of an accompanying leaflet that had been lying on the bar counter. These, the landlord had assured him, had been delivered by Bradshaw at about four p.m. on the Friday afternoon Charlotte Lambert had disappeared. He even showed the Chief Inspector the receipt Bradshaw had written out for him, also dated for that same Friday, and was willing to state on oath that, when Bradhsaw had driven away, he had not turned to the left, which would have taken him back to Dewsbury, but to the right, into the road that led through Pelham village to the T-junction.

As for Bradshaw's alibi of the phone call made by Richard Powell to the shop at about the time Charlotte Lambert disappeared, Finch thought he knew how that had been established although, at the time, Bradshaw probably had no intention of using it to cover up the murder. Simply by pressing the hache key and dialling in a special number, he had set up a call diversion system before he left for the pub, which automatically transferred any incoming calls to his mobile phone. By that means, he could speak to any clients directly, without needing to use the answer-phone. And Bradshaw had a mobile phone. It was lying on one of the counters in the back room.

When he and Helen Wyatt had sat in the car outside Print Design, waiting for the back-up team of uniformed officers to arrive from Chelmsford, they had discussed the possible scenario for that Friday afternoon, which had culminated in the abduction of and, as both agreed, the murder of Charlotte Lambert.

At about a quarter to four, Bradshaw left the shop, having dialled in the code on the phone for any calls to be diverted to his mobile and having loaded the leaflets and posters into his car. Presumably no one had seen him leave, although that would have to be established when the other shopkeepers were interviewed. Having delivered the leaflets and posters to the Lord Nelson and been paid by the landlord, Bradshaw had then driven away, not back to Dewsbury but in the opposite direction. His reason for doing so had still to be established, although Finch suspected that it was one of those fatal spur-of-the-moment decisions that can have tragic consequences. It could have been nothing more than a reluctance to go back to the shop on such a warm summer afternoon. As Mrs Bradshaw had explained, when Finch had first interviewed her, her husband wasn't completely reconciled to leaving London and his well-paid job and becoming self-employed in a small printing firm in a country backwater.

He may, therefore, have simply decided to bunk off for an hour or so by not driving straight back to the shop but taking a round-about route that would lead eventually back to Dewsbury. He may even have intended to call in on the way at home for a tea break with his wife.

All of this would, of course, have to be confirmed with Bradshaw during his interview with him at Divisional Headquarters.

So Bradshaw sets off up the road away from Dewsbury, turning left at the T-junction into Pelham Lane, which would have taken him past the farm. The time would have been roughly about 4.15, and Mrs Conway would have left her gardening and gone into the house to make tea in the kitchen to the rear of the building. Therefore, when Bradshaw drove past, she would neither have seen nor heard his car. Conway and Jessop would have not seen or heard anything either as both were busy tending to the pigs some distance away.

At the bottom of Pelham Lane, Bradshaw would have had to stop in order to check that no traffic was travelling along the Foxton road, his intention probably being to turn left and follow the road into Foxton itself. But he changed his mind at the sight of Charlotte Lambert, walking down the road towards Northorpe.

God knows what went through his mind. Finch doubted if, at this point, Bradshaw had any intention of harming her in any way, let alone murdering her. Seeing her, he probably wanted simply to give her a lift home. So he turned right and drew up alongside her.

She would, of course, have accepted the offer of a lift without any hesitation. She knew Bradshaw; he was the father of her schoolfriend; he could communicate easily with her in sign language; he represented no threat whatsoever.

At this point Finch's imagination failed him. He had no idea what happened next to set Bradshaw on the course to murder. It could have been something quite simple. An inadvertent gesture by the girl. A smile. Her hand accidentally touching his.

But something must have happened in that car to rouse Bradshaw sexually. There was no other motive that made sense of the girl's murder. He must have desired her so passionately that no other consideration mattered: not the girl's youth, nor the fact she was his own daughter's friend; that he was, in a sense, in *loco parentis*. Nothing counted except his driving urge to possess her.

Finch had closed his eyes for a moment, switching off the images, letting his mind go blank.

Only Bradshaw knew, as only he knew where he had killed her and hidden her body.

It was at this point that the SOCO team moved in with their equipment and, having directed them towards the articles that he wanted collected up for evidence, such as the mobile phone and extra copies of the leaflets and posters that were lying beside one of the copying machines in the back room, he turned to give similar instructions to the police photographer, who arrived shortly afterwards.

That done, he looked across at Helen Wyatt and nodded to her to indicate that it was time to go.

Outside, the area in front of the shop had been taped off and a couple of uniformed men were on duty to prevent the group of onlookers from approaching too close. By then, it had grown to a sizeable crowd, at the front of which stood the owner of Marilyn's. Walking across to her, he lifted the tape and invited her to step inside the cordon, which she did with alacrity, while those left behind craned and whispered together, excited at being involved, however indirectly, with a real life police investigation, just like you could see on the telly.

Marilyn was even more thrilled at being invited into the magic circle, so to speak. But the question the Detective Chief Inspector asked her was deliberately downbeat.

'Where did Mr Bradshaw normally park his car? At the back of the shop or on the forecourt?'

She looked at him for a moment, disappointed and bewildered by the banality of the question.

'Park his car?' she repeated. 'Well, round the back, of course. All of us do; I mean, all of us shopkeepers. It leaves the forecourt free for the customers and, besides, it's easier to load and unload through the back door.'

'Thank you,' Finch said with exaggerated courtesy and, escorting her back to the edge of the crowd, lifted the tape again for her to rejoin her fellows. Her brief moment centre stage was over. She was back again among the groundlings.

'Where to?' Helen asked as Finch got into the car beside her.

He hesitated for a moment. He ought, he supposed, to call on Lambert to let him know of these new developments, but he decided against it. His immediate priority was to interview Bradshaw and to get a confession of guilt out of the man, at the same time persuading him to tell them what he'd done with her body. Then he would be able to give Lambert all the answers he needed.

CHAPTER NINETEEN

It took over four hours to interview Derek
Bradshaw. For a large part of that time, he
remained mute, his features clenched shut.
Questioning him was like trying to prise open
a fist, finger by finger. It was frustrating and
exhausting. Even his own solicitor looked worn
out. Several times Finch had to leave the
interview room simply to escape from its sullen
atmosphere, which weighed heavily on his
spirits.

Outside in the corridor, he paced up and
down, stretched his spine and swung his arms
backwards and forwards, simple exercises that
he'd read somewhere helped to ease tension.
They did up to a point.

It was on his sixth return from such a
session that Bradshaw finally broke. Perhaps
his solicitor, a heavily built man whose wheezy
breathing had seemed to fill the room, had
finally persuaded him of the futility of keeping
silent any longer. Or perhaps Bradshaw
himself was exhausted by the long, drawn-out
business although it was difficult to tell what
he was feeling; his features were too rigid to
convey any emotion. Whatever the reason, the
breakthrough had been made. As Finch and
Helen Wyatt re-entered the room, the
solicitor, nodded at Finch and announced, 'Mr

Bradshaw would like to make a statement'.

The first part of it was very close to what Finch had already surmised. Bradshaw had gone to his shop in Dewsbury and, at about quarter to four in the afternoon had decided to deliver the leaflets and posters to the Lord Nelson public house, without troubling to ask his wife to come over on the bus and look after the shop as he usually did when he was making a delivery.

'I didn't bother,' he explained. 'It was only a couple of miles down the road. I wasn't going to be away all that long.'

He'd loaded up the order and, before locking up and leaving, he'd entered the code on the phone that automatically transferred any incoming calls to his mobile. Only one person had rung him—Richard Powell, at half past four and, as he usually did, he drew the car off the road and switched off the engine to take the call. But that was later, after he'd made the delivery at the Lord Nelson when, instead of going straight back to the shop as he'd intended, he'd changed his mind.

'Why?' Finch asked.

It was a minor point but one that was crucial to the sequence of events which followed. Had Bradshaw not changed his mind, Charlotte Lambert would still be alive.

Bradshaw himself looked puzzled as if he, too, was unsure of his motives, and then, after a long silence, he said, 'To be honest, I was just fed up. I've worked damned hard but, even so, I don't make a lot of profit and that morning I'd had a lot of bills in the post—the phone, the electricity, as well as a bank statement. I'd got just over five hundred quid in my account. Five hundred quid! And I still had to find the school fees in August for the new term in September. When I was working in London, I had nearly twenty thousand in savings and we lived well. We didn't have to watch every penny. So I thought, 'Oh, sod it! I'm going to have a couple of hours off.'

'I'd no intention of going to Northorpe. I just thought I'd drive about for a bit. So I set off down the road and when I came to the T-junction, I turned left instead of going straight on to Stoneleigh. I didn't know where I was until I got to the end of the lane and came to another T-junction. I realised then it joined the Foxton road so I decided I'd go home and just sit in the garden for a while and read the paper. I hadn't done that for months. Then I'd drive back to the shop.'

He stopped there and fell silent as if in his mind he was still sitting in his car at the junction of Pelham Lane and Foxton road, looking up and down to make sure the road was clear.

The silence grew louder, a ridiculous concept but to Finch it indeed seemed to become more audible. At least, noises he hadn't noticed before began to force

254

themselves on his consciousness—the faint whirr of the recording equipment, the squeak of the solicitor's chair as he shifted it on the plastic tiles on the floor, his own breathing, which sounded thunderous. And somewhere deep inside the building, the urgent clamour of a telephone.

It acted like a wake-up call on Bradshaw. He sat up suddenly and said, his eyes fixed straight ahead, 'That's when I saw her'.

'Charlotte Lambert?' Finch asked quietly.

Bradshaw appeared not to hear him. He continued, eyes still fixed on the same point on the opposite wall, 'She was walking down the road towards Northorpe. So, instead of turning left towards Foxton, as I'd intended, I turned right and caught up with her.'

He halted abruptly and his lips began to work as if mouthing the words which he could not bring himself to articulate out loud. They had reached, Finch told himself silently, that narrow window of opportunity beyond which lay murder.

'And you offered her a lift,' he suggested.

Although Bradshaw had not apparently heard Finch's remark, it must have penetrated into his consciousness at some level because he picked it up and continued with it.

'I got as far as the gate to her house. You have to get out of the car to open it so you can go up the drive. I'd stopped and she started to open the car door and signed to me that she'd walk the rest of the way. Then she signed to thank me and smiled.'

He stopped again and, turning his gaze from that one spot on the wall, he looked directly at the Chief Inspector.

'She shouldn't have smiled! Not like that! I suddenly wanted her—oh, so much I couldn't bear it.'

His voice and expression were quite wild and his eyes darted about the interview room with the desperation of an animal seeking some corner in which to hide. He seemed incapable of coherent speech and to put the man out of his misery, Finch picked up his account in a calm, almost matter-of-fact voice.

'So you drove on. Where did you take her? Did you turn back or did you go on through Northorpe?'

He doubted the last alternative. The door-to-door enquiries in the village had established the fact that several people had been out and about soon after the time that the abduction must have taken place, but no one had seen any cars apart from the local doctor's Ford, Major Roth's Rover and the Bensons' Peugeot, all of them well known in the village and all of them out on legitimate business which had been checked.

So he must have gone back along the Foxton road, Finch assumed and was considerably taken aback by Bradshaw's next remark.

Speaking as if he had not heard Finch's remark, he continued, 'I took her up that lane, the one on the right just past Lambert's house. She was struggling to get out of the car and I was frightened.'

He was frightened!

At first it seemed an outrageous remark for Bradshaw to make but after a moment's thought Finch understood what Bradshaw meant. He had reached the point of no return. He was committed to murder. If he didn't kill her, he was facing a prison sentence for abduction, resulting in financial ruin and the destruction of his and his family's lives.

Bradshaw was saying, 'There's an opening about a couple of miles up the lane to some woods and I turned in there and tried . . .'

He broke off.

'Tried to rape her.' Finch finished the sentence as Bradshaw seemed incapable of putting into words what had happened next.

'She was still crying out,' Bradshaw went on. 'Such terrible cries! She was deaf, you know, so she couldn't make proper noises and I couldn't bear to listen. So I put my hand over her mouth to keep her quiet.' A long pause followed before he added quite simply, 'She stopped breathing'.

A great stillness fell over the room. No one seemed to know what to do or say. Helen Wyatt remained immobile apart from her hands, which clasped and unclasped as they lay on the table. Dorney, Bradshaw's solicitor, was staring straight ahead, his bottom teeth nibbling away at his lip. As for Bradshaw, he sat like a man exhausted, his head hanging low, his hands dangling loose between his knees. It was as if a spell had fallen over all of them.

It was Finch who broke it. Still speaking in that flat, matter-of-fact voice, he asked, 'What did you do with her body, Mr Bradshaw?'

The man's head jerked up.

'I drove a bit further up the path into the wood. Then I carried her into some bushes and covered her over with branches.'

'Where exactly?'

Bradshaw blinked and hesitated as if unwilling to commit himself. What the hell was he thinking? That Charlotte Lambert's body could stay hidden for ever, like dust swept under a carpet?

'On the right,' he said at last. 'There's a sort of a dip in the ground.'

So at last, thank God, they knew where to look for the body.

What happened next was accounted for later in Bradshaw's official statement. He had driven on along to a T-junction where the lane joined the by-pass, the same route Lambert had taken when he had driven to Colchester, although neither Bradshaw nor Finch were aware of this. At the T-junction, he had turned left towards Foxton, not right in the direction of Colchester. The time was then about half past five and, instead of going back to the shop, he had driven for another half an hour or so round the area before going home. There had been, in fact, no need to return to Dewsbury. The shop was locked up; no lights were left on; the Closed sign was hanging in the door. His wife had been a little surprised to see him home so early—it was usually nearer eight o'clock before he closed the shop—but he made the excuse that he felt unwell and escaped to bed.

More crucially in Finch's opinion was the remark Bradshaw made at the very end of his statement. It was an attempt, the Chief Inspector thought, to excuse the murder and to evoke their sympathy, although Helen Wyatt, who was taking down the statement as a back-up to the recording of it, kept her expression perfectly blank. As for Finch, he simply looked away.

'You see,' Bradshaw said, 'I was under a lot of stress, what with all those bills coming in and not enough money to cover Fiona's bloody school fees.'

Bradshaw was almost certainly unaware of what this part of his statement revealed.

The motive was primarily not sexual although this certainly played an important part in Charlotte Lambert's murder. More relevant, Finch thought, was a deeply held resentment against his own daughter—for

259

being deaf and, because of that handicap, for being the cause of his having to give up his job in London and move to Essex so that she could go to a private school, the fees for which he couldn't really afford. Although Bradshaw himself was probably unaware of it and would deny it vigorously if he was ever confronted by it, Charlotte Lambert had been killed as a scapegoat for his own daughter.

CHAPTER TWENTY

It wasn't until early evening that Finch was free to drive to Northorpe to see Alex Lambert. He felt a little guilty about the delay in getting in touch with the man to inform him that his daughter's killer had been charged and her body found only a short time before in a wood just off Drover's Lane.

He had gone in his own car to take part in the search for Charlotte Lambert's body, a decision he had made without fully examining his reasons for it, although, at the back of his mind, he had already decided that he wanted to be alone with Lambert when he broke the news to him.

As for the girl's body, it was quickly discovered. It lay, as Bradshaw had described, to the right of a bridleway, not far from the road, in a natural declivity in the ground and was covered with bracken and branches. The reason Stapleton's men hadn't discovered it in their own searches was the fact that it lay just beyond the half mile limit that had been set outside the village which, ironically, would have been extended to a mile the following week.

As the discovery was made, Finch stood a little distance away, watching as the police surgeon pronounced her dead and the photographer moved about as if taking part in a ritual dance. The bright light from the flash camera and steady beam from the arc lamps set up for the benefit of the video camera, underlit the leaves on the trees and gave them an unearthly brilliance, blotting out the gentler glow of the late afternoon sunlight. A little further off, the hazard lights of the mortuary van, parked in the bridleway, were pulsing on and off, adding a more urgent signal like a rapid heartbeat.

Standing there, watching the figures moving to and fro, Finch breathed in the scents of the wood, the green tang of crushed grass, the earthy aroma of disturbed leaf-mould, the mushroomy odour of damp soil. He made no attempt to move nearer to the scene. When he had arrived, he had taken a rapid glance at the body when it was first uncovered but had protected himself from absorbing too much detail by deliberately censoring the normal process of observation and allowing only a limited number of images to impress themselves on his vision, and even these were incomplete: a mere glimpse of a blue and white striped dress, a strand of light brown hair, the curve of a cheek spattered with soil and leaf debris.

The SOCOs were erecting a plastic tent over the hollow in the ground, where they would work inspecting the scene and the pathologist would make an initial examination of the body. They could be there for hours. In the meantime, there was the living to consider.

Finch nodded to Helen Wyatt and, murmuring something about seeing her later back at headquarters, he set off for the lane where he had parked his car.

It took only a few minutes to drive to Lambert's house, where he was surprised to find the gate was set open. Someone must have left without taking the trouble to close it. Not Lambert, Finch surmised. He was the sort of man so obsessed with his privacy that he would make sure any access to his house or garden was sealed off. So he must have had a visitor. Finch wondered who.

Parking the car outside the front door, he gave three slow knocks, followed by two rapid ones. No one came. He knocked again and then a third time but when the door still remained closed, he tried peering through the letterbox but saw only a narrow view of the empty hall. Stepping back, he examined the front of the house. As usual, the blinds were drawn over the downstairs windows.

Baffled, he walked round to the side of the house to look up at the attic window in the gable end. That was closed; so, too, was the back door when he tried that. There remained only the garage, nothing more than a large wooden shed with double doors, that stood on its own concrete apron under some trees a little distance from the house.

It was unlocked, the padlock dangling from the hasp, the doors left half-open. As for the garage, it was empty, the only evidence that a car had stood there was a patch of blackened oil on the concrete floor.

Lambert had clearly left in his car, although there were signs that someone, presumably Lambert, had made a hurried search of the place. The top drawer of an old chest of drawers standing against the back wall, which clearly used to house small tools and bits and pieces such as screws and nails, was pulled open and some of its contents were scattered about on the floor. A reel of green plastic hosepipe lay nearby on its side.

For some reason he couldn't quite define, Finch felt uneasy, although he told himself there was no obvious cause for it. Lambert had simply driven off somewhere, to Chelmsford, perhaps, or to Colchester to go to his bank or call on one of his clients. He'd be back soon enough and, once he'd returned, he could tell him about the latest developments in the case.

It was a damned nuisance he'd disconnected his phone. It would have been so easy to have rung him up and arranged to meet him. He could, of course, send him an email but it seemed an impersonal way to communicate the news that his daughter's body had been found and her murderer arrested. He preferred to talk to him face to face if possible. To do so, though, meant calling again at the house and, with so much on his own plate at the moment, it wouldn't be easy to find the time.

Shrugging his shoulders with impatience at Lambert for being so annoyingly inaccessible and at himself for being so concerned about it, he stumped out of the garage, closing the double doors behind him and, getting into the car, drove down to the gate which he also took the trouble to shut, God knows why; perhaps as a form of recompense for the man's daughter lying dead in that shallow grave under the trees.

In the event, it was three days before he found the time to return to Field Lodge. Before that, there was the PM on Charlotte Lambert's body to attend, not a duty he took any pleasure in. The murder alone was bad enough; the dissection of her body a desecration; necessary, of course; not that it made it any better.

The outcome was what he had expected, given Bradshaw's confession. Death was due to asphyxia, the bruising around the jaw and mouth suggesting that she had been manually suffocated. There were also signs of attempted rape from the bruises and scratches on the inner thighs, but penetration had not taken place. The hymen was intact. It was a small mercy but one for which Finch was profoundly grateful.

No sooner than the PM was completed than

Jocelyn Harvey rang Divisional Headquarters in some considerable distress to report that Noel Murray was missing. Finch was out and the sergeant who took the call passed it on to the Chief Inspector who, suspecting she was the type of woman who dramatised quite ordinary situations to draw attention to herself, sent Kyle and a uniformed constable to the house to make enquiries, fully expecting that Murray had merely gone away for a few days.

He was surprised, therefore, when Kyle phoned in to report that Murray's car was in the garage and, more disturbingly, the patio doors in the drawing room were open, the curtains were partly drawn and lights had been left on in there as well as other parts of the house.

Accompanied by Helen Wyatt, Finch drove over to The Lawns, where he met Kyle, who further reported that he'd made a cursory search of the house and found Murray's passport; his wallet, containing his credit cards; his chequebook and his mobile phone, which had been left on top of the bureau in the main bedroom, as if Murray had emptied his pockets on returning home. There was no sign that he had left in a hurry, as the unlocked patio doors and lights still burning on might suggest. Nothing in the bedroom was disturbed. Drawers were tidy, clothes hung in neat rows in the wardrobe, shoes lined up below them on racks. He apparently hadn't packed in a panic.

Lambert gone and now Murray. It was an odd coincidence, although there might be a perfectly simple explanation for Murray's disappearance. The man could be in financial trouble again and had decided to make a bolt for it. But in that case, why had he left his car behind and his wallet?

Leaving Kyle and a WPC to interview Jocelyn Harvey, who might know of an address where Murray had gone to, he arranged for the house to be secured and a uniformed PC to be left on duty. As for himself, there was someone nearer home who might have the answer to Murray's sudden disappearance.

'Let's try Lambert's place,' he told Helen Wyatt.

As usual, he had to climb out of the car to open the gate at Field Lodge, but this time, instead of getting back into the car, he waved Helen on and walked up the drive to the house.

It looked, he thought, curiously empty, although there was nothing positive about the place to suggest it was vacant. Like the last time he had called there, the blinds were drawn on the downstairs windows and no one answered either the front or the back door. The garage doors remained exactly as he had left them, the padlock hanging loosely from the hasp. The garage itself was still empty.

267

Baffled, he stood on the concrete apron, arms folded, wondering what to do next. The disappearance of the two men had to be connected in some way. It was too damned coincidental for both of them to have shoved off without telling anyone; Lambert in particular, who had every reason to stay. Neither his daughter's body nor her killer had been found at the time he'd left. Surely he wouldn't have disappeared without waiting for news?

Lambert and Murray. Murray and Lambert.

What the hell was the connection between them?

Could there have been a rivalry between them over Jocelyn Harvey? It was possible, he supposed. Perhaps she'd been Lambert's lover and Murray had taken her from him, although Finch didn't care much for this theory. He couldn't imagine Lambert having an affair with Jocelyn Harvey. She was too obvious; not Lambert's type at all, he would have imagined. But there had to be some reason why the two men had disappeared at roughly the same time.

Setting aside the Lambert-Murray-Jocelyn theory, Finch wondered if Lambert had murdered Murray for some other reason and had cleared off before the crime was discovered.

It had to be that way round—that Lambert was the murderer and Murray the victim. The fact that Murray's car was still in his garage pointed in that direction. If Murray was the killer, he would have needed the car to dispose of the body and make his escape.

Finch pulled himself up suddenly.

For God's sake, the scenario was way over the top! It would amount to yet another abduction and murder, followed by the concealment of the body. Was that feasible? Common sense told him no. And yet his intuition whispered in his ear that some crime had been committed.

The only other theory that occurred to him was that the disappearance of both men was in some way connected with Charlotte Lambert's disappearance and murder. It certainly could have made more sense earlier on in the enquiry but now that Bradshaw had confessed to the girl's murder, that theory no longer held any water.

There was also the question of where the two men had disappeared to. With no car, Murray couldn't have gone far unless he'd hired one or used the train. He'd need a taxi, though, to get to Chelmsford station. DCs Barnaby and Waterhouse could check out taxis and car hire firms. As for Lambert, he'd got his car so he could be anywhere in the country. He might even have gone abroad.

But wherever he was, Jocelyn Harvey was as much in the dark as the Chief Inspector.

It was not until three weeks later that a part,

at least, of the mystery was solved. A report from Warwickshire police arrived, informing him that a body had been found in a car parked in a wood near the village of Kedstone. Through the car's registration, the owner, Peter Alexander Lambert, had been traced to an address in Essex. Further enquiries had established the fact that a Mr Lambert had been reported missing. Would Detective Chief Inspector Finch make arrangements for someone to travel to Warwickshire to identify the body?

Finch set out by car with Helen Wyatt at the wheel as soon as he could find someone to cover for him during his absence. Inspector Russell of Warwickshire CID, whom they met in Warwick at Headquarters, then drove them about ten miles out of the city to a wood, Hangman's Grove, as Russell explained on the way there; a suitably macabre name for the site of Lambert's suicide, although the wood itself was beautiful, a calm, green place of bracken and ancient oak trees standing in small grassy glades.

Lambert's car had been found under a large oak tree in one of these clearings, some distance from a public footpath and, judging by the swathe of damaged vegetation, had been driven like a tank through the undergrowth to this particular spot, God alone knew why. Inspector Russell could offer no explanation. There were several other sites more easily accessible than this one. Of course, its isolation might have been the reason why Lambert chose it. Certainly, it seemed to explain why the car had not been found for three weeks which, judging by the state of the body, was the length of time Lambert had been dead.

There was no suicide note but the assumption that he had killed himself seemed to be borne out by the evidence. A length of green plastic garden hose had been attached to the exhaust pipe with gaffer tape and fed through the boot of the car into its interior, the other end coming to rest under the driver's seat. Apparently, the engine had been left running. The ignition was still turned on when the car was found, but the petrol had long since run out.

Seeing the plastic hose and the gaffer tape, Finch realised the significance of the evidence he had noticed in Lambert's garage without realising its importance at the time. The hose-reel lying overturned and the drawer in the tool chest left open, some of its contents scattered on the floor, drew him to the conclusion that, before driving away, Lambert had searched hurriedly for the tape and perhaps also for a knife with which to cut off a length of hose. His suicide, therefore, had been planned, and was not a spur-of-the-moment act of despair.

'But why Kedstone?' Finch asked Russell.

'As far as we know, Lambert had been living in Manchester before he moved to Northorpe. He had no connections with this particular Warwickshire village.'

Russell shrugged. 'We think his father was the vicar here some years ago. The man's dead now, of course; the father I mean. That may have been the reason he came back here to die. Perhaps the place had happy memories for him as a child.'

Finch merely grunted. He wasn't too sure about this explanation but there seemed no other reason why he should have chosen to drive all those miles to this out-of-the-way spot unless it had some special significance for him.

Had he really been happy here?

Finch glanced about him. He had never much cared for woods himself, finding them dank and full of brambles and the smell of rotting vegetation. By now, the light was fading rapidly and the scene had taken on a sinister air. The trees crowded too close, shutting out the last of the light, and he could feel the damp rising through the soles of his shoes. Hangman's Grove. It seemed an apt name for the place.

He turned back to Russell.

'Could we take a look at the village on the way back?' he asked.

'Of course,' the Inspector replied, adding a little defensively, 'It's not much of a place . . .'

And he was right. There was very little to

recommend Kedstone. It had a few houses, a pub, a church with a flint tower and, close to it, the vicarage where presumably Lambert had grown up. It was a Victorian building of dark brick and slate, surrounded by trees, and looked grim in Finch's opinion. He imagined it would be hell living in it in the winter. One light shone at a downstairs window. Apart from that, the rest of the façade was in darkness.

Later, looking down at Lambert's face in the mortuary at Warwick hospital, he wondered again what had gone through the man's mind as he got in his car and set off on that last journey.

Going home.

Is that what he had thought?

To Finch, the phrase was full of a poignant longing, a sort of nostalgia—for what? He himself wasn't too sure. He only knew that certain sights and sounds could rouse in him a yearning that seemed to gnaw at his entrails. It needn't be much: the urgent flight of homing birds at twilight; smoke rising from a chimney of an isolated house; a lone figure walking along a country road; all of them glimpsed at dusk.

Home.

Russell was asking anxiously, 'Can you identify him as Peter Alexander Lambert, sir?'

Finch returned his gaze momentarily to the face of the man he had known as Alex

273

Lambert. He had been dead for three weeks, during which time he had been shut up in a car in daytime temperatures in the high seventies. Decomposition had inevitably set in; so, too, had maggot infestation. Apart from the hair and the beard, which were the same colour and texture as Lambert's as he remembered them, he couldn't be sure about the rest of the face. As for the body, that, thank God, was concealed beneath a sheet.

He averted his face.

'Sorry,' he said. 'I think it's Lambert but I can't be sure.'

'What about family?' Russell asked.

'I don't think he had any. There was only a daughter and she's dead.'

'Friends?'

Finch thought of Jocelyn Harvey and dismissed her at once. How the hell could he submit her to such an ordeal? Besides, she probably wouldn't be able to recognise him anyway.

'I don't think he had any friends,' he replied abruptly. 'Lambert was something of a recluse. You'll have to rely on dental records or fingerprints, if you can manage to take them. I'll arrange a search of his papers for the name of his dentist and doctor, and pass them on. Is that the lot?'

He was aching to get away.

'Just one more thing you may be able to help us with,' Russell said apologetically. 'A

274

photograph was found in his wallet. Perhaps you could identify it. I've got it in my office.'

But even that defeated Finch. It was a snapshot of a group of people taken in the Sixties, judging by the clothes. They were standing in a garden against a background of shrubbery and a circle had been drawn in black ink round the head of one of the men. Even without that emphasis, he would have been easily distinguishable from the rest of the group. He was standing a little in front of the others, his right foot and shoulder thrust forward as if to make sure he was the most prominent individual among them.

Finch examined his face closely. He was young, good-looking in a boyish manner, hair flopping over his forehead, the smile a little too wide. He recognised the type. A show off, he decided, a ladies' man; over-confident and probably untrustworthy. The ink circle round his head extended upwards as a straight line to the top of the photograph where a single capital letter had been added. It was an M, presumably an initial of the man's Christian or surname. But even that was no help in identifying who he was or what connection he might have had with Lambert.

However, the M bothered Finch a little. It was, he realised, the first letter of Murray's surname.

Was it significant or was it merely a coincidence? But whatever it was, it took him back to the riddle of the dual connection that had worried him before. Lambert/Murray. Murray/Lambert.

He was aware that Russell was looking at him, curious about his long silence, and he hastened to find something to say.

'I'm sorry I can't help you with the photo, but I'll make sure Mr Lambert's house is thoroughly searched for the details of his dentist,' he said. 'I'll get on to it straight away.'

It was too late to do anything that evening, he decided, when he arrived back at headquarters, but the following morning he made good his promise. Using the keys found in Lambert's pocket, a team of SOCOs went to the house and began the search, not just for the dentist's name and address but for any other documents that might throw light on the man's suicide. Although Lambert was organised as far as his professional work as an architect was concerned, there was a lot of paperwork connected with it. A four-drawer filing cabinet in the ground-floor studio was full of correspondence, copies of plans, invoices, and emails. His private papers were less carefully ordered, apart from a drawerful of letters from his daughter, which were arranged in a date sequence. The names and addresses of Lambert's doctor and dentist were soon found, filed under the general heading of Personal Information.

Finch joined the search when it was almost

finished. No suicide note had been found and nothing of any relevance to Murray that might explain the man's connection with Lambert and his subsequent disappearance. The SOCO team were preparing to call it a day when Finch turned up.

'Done and dusted down here and in the bedrooms,' Patterson reported. 'There's only the attic left. Do you want that searched as well?'

Finch hesitated. It could be an utter waste of time. On the other hand, he hated to leave any job unfinished. In the end, the desire for completion won and he nodded agreement, remembering the glimpse he'd caught of Lambert at the attic window. The man had evidently made use of the place.

More use, in fact, than Finch had anticipated, as he discovered a little later when he clambered up the folding metal ladder that gave access to the roof space through an opening in the landing ceiling.

The SOCOs had gone ahead of him and, because of the restricted space, Finch stayed on the ladder rather than join them. His head was level with the attic floor, giving him a good general view of the place. It was not as dark as he'd imagined, the window in the gable end letting in plenty of light, enabling him to see quite clearly. The floor was boarded, he noticed, and the rafters were covered with sheets of varnished hardboard, presumably for insulation and to prevent dust from sifting down from under the tiles. The general effect was pleasant, like a cabin in an old wooden sailing ship, an impression borne out by the way in which the limited space had been utilised with built-in cupboards and shelving. Like the rooms downstairs, there was minimal furniture, nothing more than a folding table and a chair set under the window with an adjacent shelf, on which were arranged an electric kettle, a jar of coffee granules, a portable radio and a CD player. CDs were neatly stacked beside it.

It reminded Finch of a schoolboy's den. He'd had one himself years ago; an old, semi-derelict shed, which he'd made weatherproof and had decorated the walls with pictures of film stars cut from magazines; ones of Deanna Durbin, he remembered, and James Mason, Margaret Lockwood and Hedy Lamarr.

Like Lambert, he'd found the means to make tea, in his case a tin kettle over an open fire behind the shed. It was where he had kept his comics and a small stock of treasures, among them a Swiss army knife, a flint arrowhead he'd picked up in a field, a cigarette lighter he'd found on the bus and one of those little machines for making roll-ups. The tobacco, stolen from his father's pouch, and the packet of cigarette papers had been kept in an airtight tin that had once held cough sweets.

During these few moments of vivid recall, he felt very close to Lambert and genuinely regretted his death.

The SOCOs had already begun their search, opening cupboards and drawers, laying out their contents on the countertops and he retreated down the ladder, leaving them to their task.

He was out of the office for the rest of the day and it was Helen Wyatt who took the phone call from Patterson, in charge of the SOCO team. A folder of manuscript pages, some sort of journal it seemed, had been found at the back of one of the cupboards, written apparently by Lambert because the handwriting matched that found among Lambert's personal papers downstairs in his office.

What should he do with it? Patterson had asked.

Knowing Finch was looking for any evidence on Lambert's connection with Murray and wondering if the so-called journal might supply it, she arranged for it to be delivered to her at Divisional Headquarters.

Flicking quickly through it, she estimated it was about forty thousand words long and, aware that Finch had enough paperwork on his plate already, with the preparation for the trial of Derek Bradshaw as well as a new case of fraud that had already landed on his desk, she rang his office and, finding he had returned, offered to transcribe it on to disc and print off a copy for easier reading. He accepted with alacrity, not expecting any come-back from her until the following morning.

He was surprised, therefore, when she came personally to his office an hour later, the folder in question in her hand, looking uncharacteristically flustered.

'What is it?' he asked.

Something had clearly happened to distress her. She was usually very much in control of herself.

She spoke quickly, rattling off the explanation in a tattoo of words.

'It's Murray, sir. Before he committed suicide, Alex Lambert abducted him and locked him up in that grotto in the gardens of Northorpe Hall. He's been there for over three weeks.'

Finch was already on his feet, thrusting his arms into the sleeves of his jacket as he made for the door.

'Round up Kyle and Williams! And phone Dr Paget. Tell him to meet us there. And get Willard to contact the hospital and tell them to have an ambulance standing by. Also the security firm to unlock those bloody gates!'

He was halfway down the stairs as he gave the final instruction and turned briefly at the bottom to add over his shoulder, 'I'll see you at the car. I want to check we have bolt cutters on board just in case.'

Shortly afterwards, as they set off for Northorpe in two cars, sirens wailing to clear a path through the home-going traffic, he was able to think more calmly.

Three weeks without food! But there was water, thank God. He remembered the little cascade pattering down the rear wall of the grotto. Yes, there was water. Murray should be all right.

He recalled the grotto: the smell of it, the liquid sounds, the sunlight shifting across the rocky surfaces. And the statue of the girl.

In a flash of intuitive connection with Lambert, he knew why he'd taken Murray there. Believing Murray was guilty, it was to punish him for his daughter's murder. The situation suddenly made sense, at least from Lambert's point of view.

He thought, too, of the waste—of life and love and forgiveness, and the pity of it. Yes, more than anything else, of the pity of it all.

We hope you have enjoyed this Large
Print book. Other Chivers Press or
Thorndike Press Large Print books are
available at your library or directly from the
publishers.

For more information about current and
forthcoming titles, please call or write,
without obligation, to:

Chivers Large Print
published by BBC Audiobooks Ltd
St James House, The Square
Lower Bristol Road
Bath BA2 3BH
UK
email: bbcaudiobooks@bbc.co.uk
www.bbcaudiobooks.co.uk

OR

Thorndike Press
295 Kennedy Memorial Drive
Waterville
Maine 04901
USA
www.gale.com/thorndike
www.gale.com/wheeler

All our Large Print titles are designed for
easy reading, and all our books are made to
last.